ALSO BY PAULO COELHO

The Alchemist

The Pilgrimage

The Valkyries

By the River Piedra I Sat Down and Wept

The Fifth Mountain

Veronika Decides to Die

Warrior of the Light: A Manual

Eleven Minutes

The Zahir

The Devil and Miss Prym

The Witch of Portobello

Brida

The Winner Stands Alone

Aleph

Manuscript Found in Accra

ADULTERY

ADULTERY

a novel

PAULO COELHO

Translated from the Portuguese by Margaret Jull Costa and Zoë Perry

ALFRED A. KNOPF NEW YORK 2014

THIS IS A BORZOI BOOK
PUBLISHED BY ALFRED A. KNOPF

www.aaknopf.com

Library of Congress Cataloging-in-Publication Data
Coelho, Paulo.
[Adultério. English]
Adultery: a novel / by Paulo Coelho; translated by Margaret Jull
Costa and Zoë Perry.—First United States edition.
pages cm

"Originally published in Brazil as Adultério by Sextante,
Rio de Janeiro, in 2012"—Title page verso.
I. Costa, Margaret Jull, translator. II. Perry, Zoë, translator.
III. Title.
PQ9698.13.O3546A3813 2014
869.3'42 dc23 2014018191

Knopf Open-Market ISBN 978-1-101-87417-2

Front-of-jacket image © Ingram Publishing
Jacket design by Compañía (lookatcia.com)

Manufactured in the United States of America
First International Edition

O Mary, conceived without sin, pray for those who turn to you. Amen.

Put out into the deep and let down your nets for a catch.

—LUKE 5:4

ADULTERY

EVERY morning, when I open my eyes to the so-called "new day," I feel like closing them again, staying in bed, and not getting up. But I can't do that.

I have a wonderful husband who is not only madly in love with me, but also the owner of a large investment fund. Every year—much to his distaste—he appears in *Bilan* magazine's list of the three hundred richest people in Switzerland.

I have two children who are (as my friends say) my "reason for living." I get up early to make their breakfast and take them on the five-minute walk to school, where they spend all day, allowing me to work and fill my time. After school, a Filipino nanny looks after them until my husband and I get home.

I enjoy my work. I'm a highly regarded journalist at a respectable newspaper that can be found in almost all the news kiosks in Geneva, where we live.

Once a year, I go on holiday with the whole family, usually to some far-flung paradise with marvelous beaches, where we stay in exotic cities inhabited by very poor people who make us feel richer, more privileged, and more grateful for the blessings life has bestowed upon us.

Ah, but I haven't introduced myself. Pleased to meet you. My name's Linda. I'm in my thirties, five-foot-eight, 150 pounds, and I wear the best clothes that money can buy (thanks to my husband's limitless generosity). I arouse desire in men and envy in other women.

And yet, every morning, when I open my eyes to this ideal life that everyone dreams of having but few achieve, I know the day will be a disaster. Until the beginning of this year, I didn't question anything. I simply got on with my life, although, now and then, I did feel guilty about having more than I deserved. One day, though, while I was making everyone breakfast (it was spring, I remember, and the flowers were just beginning to open in the garden), I asked myself: "Is this it?"

I shouldn't have asked that question. It was all the fault of a writer I'd interviewed the previous day who, at one point, said:

"I haven't the slightest interest in being happy. I prefer to live life passionately, which is dangerous because you never know what might happen next."

At the time, I thought: "Poor man. He's never satisfied. He'll die sad and embittered."

The following day, I realized that I never take any risks at all.

I know what lies ahead of me: another day exactly like the previous one. And passion? Well, I love my husband, which means that I've no cause to get depressed over living with someone purely for the sake of his money, the children, or to keep up appearances.

I live in the safest country in the world, I have no problems to speak of, and I'm a good wife and mother. I was brought up as a strict Protestant and intend to pass that education on to my children. I never take a false step because I know how easy it is to ruin everything. I do what I have to do efficiently and put as little of myself into it as possible. When I was younger, I experienced the pain of unrequited love, just like any other normal person.

Since I married, though, time has stopped.

Until, that is, I came across that horrible writer and his answer to my question. I mean, what's wrong with routine and boredom?

To be honest, nothing at all. It's just . . . it's just the secret fear that everything could change from one moment to the next, catching me completely unawares.

From the moment I had that ominous thought that bright, beautiful morning, I began to feel afraid. Would I be capable of facing the world alone if my husband died? "Yes," I told myself, because the money he left behind would be enough to support several generations. And if I died, who would look after my children? My beloved husband. But he would surely remarry, because he's rich, charming, and intelligent. Would my children be in good hands?

The first thing I did was try to answer all my questions. And the more questions I answered, the more questions appeared. Will he take a mistress when I get old? We don't make love as often as we used to—does he already have someone else? Does he think *I've* found someone else because I haven't shown much interest in sex for the last three years?

We never have jealous spats, and I used to think that was great, but after that spring morning, I began to suspect that perhaps our lack of jealousy meant a complete lack of love on both sides.

I did my best not to think about the matter anymore.

For a whole week, whenever I left work, I would go and buy something in one of the expensive shops on Rue du Rhône. There was nothing I really wanted, but at least I felt that I was—how should I say this?—changing something, discovering something I didn't even know I needed, like some new domestic appliance, although it has to be said, novelties in the world of domestic appliances are few and far between. I avoided toy shops, because I didn't want to spoil my children by giving them a present every day. I didn't go into any men's shops, either, just in case my husband might grow suspicious of my sudden extreme generosity.

When I got home and entered the enchanted realm of my domestic world, everything would seem marvelous for a few hours, until everyone went to bed. Then, slowly, the nightmare would begin.

I think that passion is strictly for the young. Presumably, its absence is normal at my age, but that isn't what terrifies me.

Today I am a woman torn between the terror that everything might change and the equal terror that everything might carry on exactly the same for the rest of my days. Some people say that, as summer approaches, we start to have weird ideas; we feel smaller because we spend more time out in the open air, and that makes us aware of how large the world is. The horizon seems farther away, beyond the clouds and the walls of our house.

That may be true, but I just can't sleep anymore, and it isn't because of the heat. When night comes and no one is watching, I feel afraid of everything: life, death, love or the lack of it; the fact that all novelties quickly become habits; the feeling that I'm wasting the best years of my life in a pattern that will be repeated over and over until I die; and sheer panic at facing the unknown, however exciting and adventurous that might be.

Naturally, I seek consolation in other people's suffering.

I turn on the TV and watch the news. I see endless reports about accidents, people made homeless by natural disasters, refugees. How many people on the planet are ill right now? How many, whether in silence or not, are suffering injustices and betrayals? How many poor people are there, how many unemployed or imprisoned?

I change channels. I watch a soap or a movie and for a few minutes or hours I forget everything. I'm terrified my husband might wake up and ask: "What's wrong, babe?" Because then I would have to say that everything's fine. It would be even worse if—as happened a few times last month—he put his hand on my thigh, slid it slowly upward and started caressing me. I can fake orgasms—I often have—but I can't just *decide* to get wet with excitement.

I would have to say that I'm really tired, and he, never for one moment admitting that he was annoyed, would give me a kiss, turn over, and watch the latest news on his tablet, waiting until the next day. And then I would hope against hope that when the next day comes, he'd be tired. Very tired.

It's not always like that, though. Sometimes I have to take the initiative. If I reject him two nights in a row, he might go looking for a mistress, and I really don't want to lose him. If I masturbate beforehand, then I'm ready and everything's normal again.

"Normal" means that nothing will ever be as it was in the days when we were still a mystery to each other.

Keeping the same fire burning after ten years of marriage seems a complete impossibility to me. And each time I fake an orgasm, I die a little inside. A little? I think I'm dying more quickly than I thought.

My friends tell me how lucky I am, because I lie to them and tell them that we often make love, just as they lie to me when they say that they don't know how their husbands can still be so interested in sex. They say that sex in marriage is interesting only for the first five years, and after that calls for a little "imagination." Closing your eyes and imagining your neighbor lying on top of you, doing things your husband would never dare to do. Imagining having sex with him and your husband at the same time. Imagining every possible perversion, every forbidden game.

TODAY, when I leave the house to walk the kids to school, I take a good look at my neighbor. I've never imagined having sex with him. I'd rather imagine having sex with a young reporter who works with me, the one who seems to be in a permanent state of suffering and solitude. I've never seen him try to seduce anyone, and that's what's so charming. All the women in the office have commented that "the poor thing needs someone to look after him." I reckon he knows this and is happy merely to be an object of desire, nothing more. Perhaps, like me, he has a terrible fear of taking a false step and ruining everything—his job, his family, his past and future life.

Anyway, I look at my neighbor this morning and feel like crying. He is washing his car, and I think: "Look at that, another person just like me and my husband. One day we'll be doing the same thing. Our children will have grown up and moved to another city, or even another country. We'll be retired, and will spend our time washing our cars even if we can perfectly well afford to pay someone else to do it for us. After a certain age, you have to do irrelevant things—to pass the time, to show others that your body is still in working order, to express that you still appreciate the value of money and can still carry out certain humble tasks."

A clean car won't exactly change the world, but this morning, it is the only thing my neighbor cares about. He says good morning, smiles, and goes back to his work as if he were polishing a Rodin sculpture.

I LEAVE my car at the park-and-ride (Take the bus into town! Say "No" to pollution!). I catch the usual bus and look at the same things I always look at on the way in to work. Geneva doesn't seem to have changed at all since I was a child; the grand old houses are still between the buildings put up by some mad mayor who discovered "new architecture" in the 1950s.

I miss all of this when I travel. The appalling bad taste, the absence of huge glass-and-steel towers, the lack of highways, the tree roots that push through the concrete sidewalks and trip you up, the public parks with their mysterious little wooden fences overgrown with weeds because "that's what nature is like." In short, a city that is different from others that have been modernized and lost their charm.

Here, we still say "Good morning" when we meet a stranger in the street and "Good-bye" when we leave a shop after buying a bottle of mineral water, even if we have no intention of ever going back. We still chat to strangers on the bus, even though the rest of the world thinks of the Swiss as being very discreet and reserved.

How wrong they are! But it's good that other people should think of us like that, because that way we can preserve our way of life for another five or six centuries, before the Barbarians cross the Alps with their wonderful electronic gadgets; their apartments with tiny bedrooms and large living rooms to impress the guests; their women, who wear too much makeup; their men, who talk loudly and bother the neighbors; and their teenagers, who dress rebelliously but who are secretly terrified of what their parents might think.

Let them believe that all we produce is cheese, chocolate,

cows, and cuckoo clocks. Let them believe that there's a bank on every corner in Geneva. We have no intention of changing that image. We're happy without the Barbarian hordes. We're all armed to the teeth (since military service is obligatory, every Swiss man has a rifle in his house), but you rarely hear of anyone shooting anyone else.

We're pleased that we haven't changed for centuries. We feel proud to have remained neutral when Europe sent its sons off to fight senseless wars. We're glad not to have to explain Geneva's somewhat unattractive appearance, with its fin de siècle cafés and elderly ladies strolling about the city.

To say "*we're* happy" might not be entirely true. Everyone is happy apart from me, as I travel to work wondering what's wrong.

ANOTHER day at the newspaper, trying to ferret out some interesting news other than the usual car accident, weaponless mugging, and fire (which dozens of fire engines manned by highly qualified firemen rushed to put out and flooded an old apartment. All because the neighbors were alarmed about the smoke issuing from a pot roast left too long in the oven).

Back home, there's the pleasure of cooking, the table set, and the family gathered around it, thanking God for the food we're about to receive. Another evening when, after supper, each person goes about his business—the father helping the children with their homework, the mother cleaning the kitchen, tidying the house, and putting out the money for the maid the next morning.

There are times during these months when I feel really good, when I really believe that my life makes perfect sense, that this is the role of human beings on Earth. The children feel that their mother is at peace, their father is kinder and more attentive, and the whole house seems to glow with its own light. We are an example of happiness to the rest of the street, the city, the canton—or what you might call the state—of the entire country. And then suddenly, for no reason, I get into the shower and burst into tears. I can cry there because no one can hear my sobs or ask me the question I hate most: "Are you all right?"

Yes, why shouldn't I be? Is there anything wrong with my life?

No, nothing.

Only the nights that fill me with dread.

The days I can't get excited about.

The happy images from the past and the things that could have been but weren't.

The desire for adventure never fulfilled.

The terror of not knowing what will happen to my children.

Then my thoughts start to circle negative things, always the same, as if there were a devil watching from one corner of the room, ready to leap out and tell me that what I call "happiness" is merely a passing phase, that nothing lasts. Surely I know that.

I want to change. I need to change. Today at work I got ridiculously uptight, simply because an intern took longer than usual to find the material I wanted. I'm not normally like that, but I'm gradually losing touch with myself.

It's silly to blame it all on that writer and his interview. That was months ago. He merely took the top off a volcano that could have erupted at any moment, sowing death and destruction around it. If it hadn't been him, it would have been a film, a book, or someone else I happened to talk to. I imagine that some people spend years allowing the pressure to build up inside them without even noticing, and then one day some tiny incident triggers a crisis.

Then they say: "I've had enough, I don't want this anymore."

Some commit suicide. Others get divorced. Some go to poor parts of Africa to try to save the world.

But I know myself. I know that my only reaction will be to repress my feelings until a cancer starts eating me up inside. Because I do actually believe that many illnesses are the result of repressed emotions.

I WAKE at two in the morning and lie staring up at the ceiling—something I've always hated—even though I know I have to get up early to go to work. Instead of coming up with a productive question like "What's happening to me?" I let my thoughts spiral out of control. For days now—although not that many, thank God—I've been wondering if I should go to a psychiatrist and seek help. What stops me isn't my work or my husband, but my children. They couldn't understand what I'm feeling at all.

Everything grows more intense. I think about a marriage, my marriage, in which jealousy plays no part. But we women have a sixth sense. Perhaps my husband has already met someone else and I'm unconsciously responding to that. And yet I have absolutely no reason to suspect him.

Isn't this absurd? Can it be that of all the men in the world, I have married the only one who is absolutely perfect? He doesn't drink or go out at night, and he never spends a day alone with his friends. The family is his entire life.

It would be a dream if it weren't a nightmare. Because I have to reciprocate.

Then I realize that words like "optimism" and "hope," which appear in all those self-help books that claim they'll make us more confident and better able to cope with life, are just that: words. The wise people who pronounce them are perhaps looking for some meaning in their own life and using us as guinea pigs to see how we'll react to the stimulus.

The fact is, I'm tired of having such a happy, perfect life. And that can only be a sign of mental illness.

That's what I fall asleep thinking. Perhaps I really do have a serious problem.

I HAVE lunch with a friend.

She suggests meeting at a Japanese restaurant I've never heard of, which is odd, because I adore Japanese food. She assures me that it's an excellent place, although quite some way from where I work.

It takes ages to get there. I have to take two buses and ask someone the way to the gallery, home to this supposedly "excellent" restaurant. I think the place is hideous—the décor, the paper tablecloths, the lack of any view. She's right, though. It's one of the best meals I've ever eaten in Geneva.

"I always used to eat in the same restaurant, which was okay, but nothing special," she says. "Then a friend of mine who works at the Japanese consulate suggested this one. I thought it was pretty ghastly at first, as you probably did, too. But it's the owners themselves who run the restaurant, and that makes all the difference."

It occurs to me that I always go to the same restaurants and order the same dishes. I don't even take any risks in this.

My friend is on antidepressants. That's the last thing I want to talk about, though, because I've come to the conclusion that I'm just a step away from sliding into depression and I don't want to accept that.

And precisely because it's the last thing I want to talk about, it's the very first subject I bring up.

I ask how she's feeling.

"Much better," she says, "although the medication can take a while to work. Once it kicks in, though, you regain your interest in life; things get back their color and flavor."

In other words, suffering has become yet another source

of income for the pharmaceutical industry. Feeling sad? Take a pill and problem solved.

I ask, very gingerly, if she would be interested in collaborating on a major article on depression for the newspaper.

"There's no point. Nowadays people share their feelings on the Internet."

What do they discuss?

"The side effects of the different medications. No one's interested in other people's symptoms, because symptoms are infectious, and you'd suddenly start feeling things you didn't feel before."

Is that all?

"No, there are meditation exercises, too, but I don't think they're much use. I only started to get better once I accepted that I had a problem."

But doesn't it help to know you're not alone? Isn't talking about depression's effects good for other people, too?

"No, not at all. If you've just emerged from hell, you don't want to know what life is like down there right now."

Why did you put up with it for so many years?

"Because I didn't believe I could be depressed. And because whenever I talked about it with you or with other friends, everyone said it was nonsense, that people with *real* problems don't have time to feel depressed."

It's true, that's exactly what I said.

I insist: Wouldn't an article or a blog help people to better cope with the illness and seek help? I'm not depressed myself, of course, and don't know how it feels. Could she tell me a bit about it?

My friend hesitates, perhaps suspicious of my motives.

"It's like being inside a trap. You know you're caught, but you can't escape . . ."

That's exactly what I felt a few days ago.

She starts listing a whole series of things that are apparently common to those who have visited what she calls "hell." Not wanting to get out of bed. Feeling that the simplest of tasks requires a Herculean effort. Being riddled with guilt because you have no reason to feel like this when there are so many people in the world who are really suffering.

I try to concentrate on the excellent food, but it has already started to lose its flavor. My friend goes on:

"Apathy. Pretending to be happy, pretending to be sad, pretending to have an orgasm, pretending to be having fun, pretending that you've slept well, pretending that you're alive. Until there comes a point where you reach an imaginary red line and realize that if you cross it, there will be no turning back. Then you stop complaining, because complaining means that you are at least still battling something. You accept the vegetative state and try to conceal it from everyone. And that's hard work."

And what caused your depression?

"Nothing in particular. But why so many questions? Are you feeling depressed, too?"

Of course not!

Best to change the subject.

We talk about the politician I'm going to interview in a couple days' time. He's an ex-boyfriend of mine from high school who probably doesn't even remember that we once exchanged a few kisses and that he touched my breasts.

My friend is thrilled. I, on the other hand, try not to think about anything, keeping my reactions set to automatic.

Apathy. I haven't yet reached that stage. I'm still at the complaining one, but I imagine that soon—in a matter of months, days, or hours—a complete lack of interest will set in that will be very hard to dispel.

It feels like my soul is slowly leaving my body and heading

off to an unknown place, some "safe" place where it doesn't have to put up with me and my night terrors. It's as if I weren't sitting in an ugly Japanese restaurant with delicious food, experiencing everything as though it were just a scene in a film I'm watching, without wanting—or being able—to stop it.

I WAKE up and perform the usual rituals—brushing my teeth, getting dressed for work, going into the children's bedroom to wake them up, making breakfast for everyone, smiling, and saying how good life is. In every minute and gesture I feel a weight I can't identify, like an animal who can't quite understand how it got caught in the trap.

My food has no taste. My smile, on the other hand, grows even wider so that no one will suspect, and I swallow my desire to cry. The light outside seems gray.

Yesterday's conversation did no good at all; I'm starting to think that I'm headed out of the indignant phase and straight into apathy.

And does no one notice?

Of course not. After all, I'm the last person in the world to admit that I need help.

This is my problem; the volcano has exploded and there's no way to put the lava back inside, plant some trees, mow the grass, and let the sheep out to graze.

I don't deserve this. I've always tried to meet everyone's expectations. But now it's happened and I can't do anything about it except take medication. Perhaps today I'll come up with an excuse to write an article about psychiatry and social security (the newspaper loves that kind of thing) and find a good psychiatrist to ask for help. I know that's not ethical, but then not everything is.

I don't have an obsession to occupy my mind—for example, dieting or being OCD and finding fault with the cleaning lady who arrives at eight in the morning and leaves at five in the afternoon, having washed and ironed the clothes, and tidied the house, and, sometimes, having even done the shopping, too. I can't vent my frustrations by trying to be Supermom, because my children would resent me for the rest of their lives.

I go off to work and again see the neighbor polishing his car. Wasn't he doing that yesterday?

Unable to resist, I go over and ask him why.

"It wasn't quite perfect," he says, but only after having said "Good morning," asking about the family, and noticing what a pretty dress I'm wearing.

I look at the car. It's an Audi—one of Geneva's nicknames is, after all, Audiland. It looks perfect, but he shows me one or two places where it isn't as shiny as it should be.

I draw out the conversation and end up asking what he thinks people are looking for in life.

"Oh, that's easy enough. Being able to pay their bills. Buying a house like yours or mine. Having a garden full of trees. Having your children or grandchildren over for Sunday lunch. Traveling the world once you've retired."

Is that what people want from life? Is it really? There's something very wrong with this world, and it isn't just the wars going on in Asia or the Middle East.

Before I go to the newspaper, I have to interview Jacob, my ex-boyfriend from high school. Not even that cheers me up. I really am losing interest in things.

I LISTEN to facts about government policy that I didn't even want to know. I ask a few awkward questions, which he deftly dodges. He's a year younger than me, but he looks five years older. I keep this thought to myself.

Of course, it's good to see him again, although he hasn't yet asked me what's happened in my life since we each went our own way after graduation. He's entirely focused on himself, his career, and his future, while I find myself staring foolishly back at the past as if I were still the adolescent who, despite the braces on my teeth, was the envy of all the other girls. After a while, I stop listening and go on autopilot. Always the same script, the same promises—reducing taxes, combating crime, keeping the French (the so-called cross-border workers who are taking jobs that Swiss workers could fill) out. Year after year, the issues are the same and the problems continue unresolved because no one really cares.

After twenty minutes of conversation, I start to wonder if my lack of interest is due to my strange state of mind. No. There is nothing more tedious than interviewing politicians. It would have been better if I'd been sent to cover some crime or another. Murderers are much more real.

Compared to representatives of the people anywhere else on the planet, ours are the least interesting and the most insipid. No one wants to know about their private lives. Only two things create a scandal here: corruption and drugs. Then it takes on gigantic proportions and gets wall-to-wall coverage because there's absolutely nothing else of interest in the newspapers.

Does anyone care if they have lovers, go to brothels, or come out as gay? No. They continue doing what they were elected to do, and as long as they don't blow the national budget, we all live in peace.

The president of the country changes every year (yes, every year) and is chosen not by the people, but by the Federal Council, a body comprising seven ministers who serve as Switzerland's collective head of state. Every time I walk past the museum, I see endless posters calling for more plebiscites.

The Swiss love to make decisions—the color of our trash bags (black came out on top), the right (or not) to carry arms (Switzerland has one of the highest gun-ownership rates in the world), the number of minarets that can be built in the country (four), and whether or not to provide asylum for expatriates (I haven't kept pace with this one, but I imagine the law was approved and is already in force).

"Excuse me, sir."

We've been interrupted once already. He politely asks his assistant to postpone his next appointment. My newspaper is the most important in French-speaking Switzerland and this interview could prove crucial for the upcoming elections.

He pretends to convince me and I pretend to believe him.

Then I get up, thank him, and say that I have all the material I need.

"You don't need anything else?"

Of course I do, but it's not up to me to tell him what.

"How about getting together after work?"

I explain that I have to pick up my children from school, hoping that he sees the large gold wedding ring on my finger declaring: "Look, the past is the past."

"Of course. Well, maybe we can have lunch someday."

I agree. Easily deceived, I think: Who knows, maybe he does have something of importance to tell me, some state secret that will change the politics of the country and make the editor look at me with new eyes.

He goes over to the door, locks it, then comes back and kisses me. I return his kiss, because it's been a long time. Jacob, whom I may have once loved, is now a family man, married to a professor. And I am a family woman, married to a man who, though he inherited his wealth, is extremely hardworking.

I consider pushing him away and saying that we're not kids anymore, but I'm enjoying it. Not only did I discover a new Japanese restaurant, I'm having a bit of illicit fun as well. I've managed to break the rules and the world hasn't caved in on me. I haven't felt this happy in a long time.

I feel better and better, braver, freer. Then I do something I've dreamed of doing since I was in school.

Kneeling down, I unzip his fly and wrap my mouth around his penis. He grabs my hair and controls the rhythm of my head. He comes in less than a minute.

"God, that was good."

I say nothing. The fact is that it was far better for me than for him, since he came so quickly.

SIN is followed by a fear of being caught.

On the way to the office, I buy a toothbrush and some toothpaste. Every half an hour or so, I go to the toilet to check that there's nothing on my face or on my Versace shirt, intricately embroidered and perfect for hiding stains. I observe my work colleagues out of the corner of my eye, but no one has noticed (or at least none of the women, who have a special radar for these things).

Why did that happen? It was as if someone else had taken over and propelled me into a situation that was purely mechanical and non-erotic. Did I want to prove to Jacob that I'm independent, free, my own woman? Did I do that in order to impress him or in an attempt to escape what my girlfriend called "hell"?

Everything will continue as before. I'm not at any crossroads. I know where I'm going and hope that, with the passing of the years, I'll manage to change my family's ways so that we don't end up thinking there's anything special about washing the car. The really big changes happen over time, and time is something of which I have plenty.

At least I hope so.

When I get home, I try to look neither happy nor sad. The children notice at once.

"You're acting funny today, Mom."

I feel like saying: Yes, I did something I shouldn't have done and yet I don't feel the tiniest bit guilty, just afraid of being found out.

My husband gets home and, as usual, he kisses me, asks what kind of day I've had and what we're having for supper. I give him the usual answers. If he doesn't notice anything different about the routine, he won't suspect that today I gave oral sex to a politician.

Which, it should be said, gave me no physical pleasure at all. But now I'm mad with desire, needing a man, needing to be kissed, and needing to feel the pain and pleasure of a body on top of mine.

When we go up to bed, I realize that I'm terribly aroused. I can't wait to make love with my husband, but I must keep calm; if I'm too eager, he'll suspect something is wrong.

After I shower, I lie down beside him, take the tablet he's reading from his hands and put it on the bedside table. I begin stroking his chest, and he immediately becomes aroused. We make love as we haven't done in a long time. When I moan a little too loudly, he asks me to keep the noise down so as not to wake the children, but I tell him I don't want to, that I want to be able to express my feelings.

I have multiple orgasms. God, I love this man! We end up sweaty and exhausted, and so I decide to take another shower. He comes in with me and playfully turns the showerhead on my clit. I ask him to stop, saying I'm too tired, that we need to sleep and he'll just get me all excited again.

While we're drying each other off, I suggest going to a nightclub sometime—another attempt to change my routine at all costs. I think it's then that he suspects something has changed.

"Tomorrow?"

I can't tomorrow, I have my yoga class.

"Since you've brought it up, can I ask a direct question?"

My heart stops. He goes on:

"Why exactly do you go to yoga classes? You're such a

calm, well-balanced person, and a woman who knows what she wants. Aren't you wasting your time?"

My heart starts beating again. I don't answer. I simply smile and stroke his face.

I collapse onto the bed, close my eyes, and, before I fall asleep, think: I must be having the kind of crisis that comes after ten years of marriage. It'll pass.

Not everyone needs to feel happy all the time. Besides, no one *can* be happy all the time. I need to learn to deal with the reality of life.

Dear Depression, please keep your distance. Don't be nasty. Find some other person with more reason than me to look in the mirror and say: "What a pointless existence." Whether you like it or not, I know how to defeat you. You're wasting your time.

MY LUNCH with Jacob König goes exactly as I imagine. We meet at La Perle du Lac, an expensive restaurant on the lakeshore that used to be good but is now owned by the city. It's still expensive, but the food is awful. I could have surprised him and taken him to the Japanese restaurant, but I know he would think it was in bad taste. For some people, décor matters more than food.

And now I see that I made the right decision. He tries to show me that he's a wine connoisseur; he talks about "bouquet," "texture," and "legs," the oily drops that fall in rivulets down the side of the glass. In truth, he's telling me that he's grown up and no longer a schoolboy; that he's learned how to behave and has risen in the world; that he knows about life, wine, politics, women, and ex-girlfriends.

What nonsense! We've been drinking wine all our lives. We can tell a good wine from a bad one, and that's all there is to it. Until I met my husband, all the men I went out with—men who considered themselves "cultivated"—acted as if the choice of wine in a restaurant was their big moment. They all did the same thing: with great solemnity, they sniffed the cork, read the label, allowed the waiter to pour a little into the glass, turned it this way and that, held it up to the light, smelled the wine, rolled it around in their mouth, swallowed, and, finally, gave an approving nod.

After witnessing the same scene endless times, I decided to change my group of friends and join the college's nerds and social outcasts. Unlike the fake, predictable tasters of wine, the nerds were at least real and made no attempt to impress me. They joked about things I didn't understand. They thought, for example, that I really ought to know the name Intel because "it's written on every computer." I, of course, had never noticed.

The nerds made me feel like a plain-Jane ignoramus, and were more interested in pirating things on the Internet than they were in my breasts or legs. As I got older, I returned to the safe embrace of the wine tasters until I found a man who didn't try to impress me with his sophistication or make me feel like a complete idiot with conversations about mysterious planets, hobbits, or computer programs that erase all traces of the webpages you've visited. After a few months of going out, during which we discovered at least one hundred and twenty villages around Lake Léman, he asked me to marry him.

I accepted without hesitation.

I ask Jacob if he knows any nightclubs, because I haven't kept up with Geneva's nightlife ("nightlife" being just a manner of speaking) and I've decided to go out dancing and drinking. His eyes shine.

"I don't have time for that. Thanks for the invitation, but, you know, apart from the fact that I'm married, I can't be seen out with a journalist. People will say your articles are . . ."

"Biased."

"Yes, biased."

I decide to take this little game of seduction a step further—it's a game that has always amused me. What have I got to lose? I know all the methods, diversions, traps, and objectives.

I ask him to tell me more about himself, about his personal life. I'm not here as a journalist, I say, but as a woman and a former girlfriend.

I stress the word "woman."

"I don't have a personal life," he says. "I can't, unfortunately. I've chosen a career that has transformed me into an automaton. Everything I say is scrutinized, questioned, published."

This isn't quite true, but I find his sincerity disarming. I know that he's mostly seeing how the land lies, that he wants to know precisely where he's putting his feet and how far he can go. He suggests that he is "unhappily married," and goes into an exhaustive explanation of how powerful he is, just like all men of a certain age once they've hit the wine.

"In the last two years I've had a few months of happiness, a few of difficulties, but most are just a matter of hanging in there and trying to please everyone in order to be reelected. I've had to give up everything that I used to enjoy—like going dancing with you, for example. Or listening to music for hours, smoking, or doing anything that other people deem to be wrong."

That's absurd! No one cares about his personal life.

"Perhaps it's the return of Saturn. Every twenty-nine years the planet returns to the same point in the sky that it occupied at the moment of our birth."

The return of Saturn?

He realizes that he's said more than he should, and suggests that it might be best if we went back to work.

No, my Saturn return has already happened. I need to know exactly what it means. He gives me a lesson in astrology: Saturn takes twenty-nine years to return to the point in the sky where it was at the moment we were born. Until that happens, everything seems possible, our dreams can come true, and any walls hemming us in can still be broken down. When Saturn completes this cycle, it puts an end to any romanticism. Choices become definitive and it's nearly impossible to change direction.

"I'm not an expert, of course, but my next chance will only come when I'm fifty-eight and Saturn returns again. Although, if Saturn is telling me it's no longer possible to choose another path, why, then, did you invite me to lunch?"

We've been talking now for almost an hour.

"Are you happy?" he asks suddenly.

What?

"There's something in your eyes, a sadness I find inexplicable in a pretty woman like you with a nice husband and a good job. It's like seeing a reflection of my own eyes. I'll ask you again: Are you happy?"

In this country where I was born and raised, and where I'm now raising my own children, *no one* asks that kind of question. Happiness is not something that can be precisely measured, discussed in plebiscites, or analyzed by specialists. We don't even ask what kind of car someone drives, let alone something so personal and impossible to define.

"There's no need to answer. Your silence says it all."

No, my silence doesn't say it all. It isn't an answer. It merely reflects my surprise and confusion.

"I'm not happy," he says. "I have everything a man could dream of, but I'm not happy."

Has someone put something in the water? Are they trying to destroy my country with a chemical weapon designed to create a sense of profound frustration? Why is it that everyone I talk to feels the same?

So far I haven't said anything. But tormented souls have this incredible ability to recognize and approach one another, thus compounding their grief.

Why hadn't I noticed this in him? Why did I see only the superficial way he talked about politics or the pedantic way he tasted the wine?

The return of Saturn. Opposition. Unhappiness. Things I never expected to hear Jacob König say.

At that precise moment—it's 1:55 p.m., according to my watch—I fall in love with him all over again. No one, not even my marvelous husband, has ever asked if I'm happy. Perhaps in my childhood, my parents and my grandparents asked that question, but no one has since.

"Shall we meet again?"

I no longer see a boyfriend from my adolescence sitting in front of me, but an abyss that I'm blithely walking toward, an abyss from which I have no desire to escape. The thought flashes through my mind that my sleepless nights are about to become even more unbearable now that I really do have a problem: a heart in love.

The red lights in my mind start to flash.

I tell myself: You're a fool, he just wants to get you into bed. He doesn't care about your happiness.

Then, in an almost suicidal gesture, I say yes. Perhaps going to bed with someone who just touched my breasts when we were teenagers will be good for my marriage, as it was yesterday, when I gave him oral sex in the morning and had multiple orgasms with my husband later that night.

I try to get back to the subject of Saturn, but he's already asked for the bill and is talking on his cell phone, saying that he'll be five minutes late.

"Ask them if they'd like a glass of water or some coffee," he says.

I ask who he was talking to, and he says it was his wife. The director of a large pharmaceutical company wants to meet and possibly invest money in the final phase of his campaign to be elected to the Council of States. The elections are fast approaching.

Again, I remember that he's married. That he's unhappy. That he can't do anything he enjoys. That there are rumors about him and his wife, that they have an open marriage. I need to forget the spark that dazzled me at 1:55 and realize that he just wants to use me.

This doesn't bother me, as long as things are clear. I, too, need someone to sleep with.

We pause on the sidewalk outside the restaurant. He looks around as if we make a highly suspicious couple. Then, when he's sure no one is looking, he lights a cigarette.

So that's what he was afraid people might see: the cigarette.

"As I'm sure you remember, I was considered the most promising student of our year," he says. "And of course I had to prove them right, what with my need for love and approval. I sacrificed nights out with my friends to study and meet other people's expectations. I finished high school with brilliant results. By the way, why did we stop going out again?"

I have no idea, either. I think at the time everyone was simply busy hooking up with everyone else, and no one stayed with anyone for very long.

"I graduated from university, became a defense lawyer, and spent my life between crooks and the completely innocent, between scoundrels and the totally honest. What started out as a temporary job became a permanent decision: a need to help. My list of clients grew and grew. My reputation spread throughout the city. My father insisted that it was time for me to give it all up and go and work in the law practice of a friend of his, but I was just too excited by each new case I won. Then I came across a completely archaic law that has absolutely no relevance today. We needed major changes in how the city was governed."

All this is in his official biography, but hearing it from his lips feels quite different.

"At one point, I decided I wanted to stand as a candidate for deputy. We campaigned with almost no money, because my father was completely opposed. But my clients were all in favor. I was elected by a tiny majority, but I was elected nonetheless."

He looks around again, having hidden the cigarette behind his back. But since no one is looking, he takes another long drag. His eyes have a vacant look as he gazes back at the past.

"When I started out in politics, I used to sleep only about five hours a night, yet I was always full of energy. Now I can easily sleep for eighteen hours at a stretch. The honeymoon is over. All that's left is my need to please others, especially my wife, who has fought like crazy for me to have a great future. Marianne has made a lot of sacrifices and I can't let her down."

Is this the same man who, only a few minutes ago, suggested that we start going out again? Or is this what he wants: someone to talk to who will understand him because she feels the same way?

I have a gift for inventing fantasies with extraordinary speed. I'm already imagining myself lying between silk sheets in some chalet in the Alps.

"So when shall we meet again?" he asks.

It's up to you, I say.

He suggests meeting on another day. I tell him that's when I have my yoga class. He asks me to skip it. But I'm always skipping it and have promised to be more disciplined.

Jacob seems resigned. I'm tempted to change my mind, but I mustn't appear too eager or too available.

Life is becoming fun again, my previous apathy replaced by fear. How wonderful it is to be afraid of missing an opportunity!

I tell him it's impossible, and that we'd better rearrange it for Friday. He accepts, phones his assistant, and asks him to put it in the diary. He finishes smoking his cigarette and says good-bye. I don't ask him why he's told me so much about his private life, and he adds nothing very significant to what he said in the restaurant.

I would like to believe that something has changed during that lunch, just one among hundreds I've had where I eat extremely unhealthy food and pretend to drink wine that remains almost untouched when the time comes to order coffee. One can never lower one's guard, despite all that fuss about tasting the wine.

The need to please everyone. Saturn in opposition.

JOURNALISM is not as glamorous as people think—it's not all interviewing famous people, being invited to amazing places, brushing shoulders with power, money, the fascinating world of criminality.

The fact is that we spend most of the time at our cubicle desks, talking on the phone. Privacy is only for the bosses, sitting in their glass aquariums, with curtains that can be occasionally closed. When they draw them, they still know what's going on outside, but we can no longer see their fish mouths moving.

Being a journalist in Geneva, with its 195,000 inhabitants, is the most boring job in the world. I glance through today's issue even though I already know what it contains—endless reports on foreign dignitary meetings at the United Nations, the usual complaints about the end to banking secrecy, and a few more things that have made it to the front page: "Morbidly Obese Man Banned from Plane," "Wolf Decimates Sheep on Outskirts of City," "Pre-Columbian Fossils Found in Saint-Georges," and, finally, in banner headlines, "Newly Restored *Genève* Returns to the Lake Looking More Beautiful Than Ever."

My boss summons me to his office and asks if I managed to get an exclusive out of my lunch with that politician. Needless to say, someone saw us together.

No, I didn't. Nothing that isn't in his official biography. The lunch was intended to get me closer to a source. (The more sources a journalist has, the more respected he or she is.)

My boss says that another reliable source has told him that, even though Jacob König is married, he's having an affair with the wife of another politician. I feel a pang in that dark corner of my soul where depression keeps knocking but I refuse to answer.

My boss asks if I can get closer. They're not particularly interested in his sex life, but *his* source suggests that König might be being blackmailed. A foreign metallurgical company wants to airbrush out certain tax problems in its own country, but has no way of getting in touch with the minister of finance. They need a little help.

My boss explains that Jacob König isn't our target; what we want is to denounce the people who are trying to corrupt our political system.

"And that shouldn't be difficult. We just have to say we're on his side."

Switzerland is one of the few countries in the world where a man's word is still his bond. In most other places you need lawyers, witnesses, signed documents, and the threat of legal process if the secret were leaked.

"We just need confirmation and photos."

So I'll need to get closer to him.

"That shouldn't be difficult, either. Our sources tell us that you've already arranged another meeting. It's in his diary."

And this is the land of banking secrecy! Everyone knows everything.

"Use the usual tactics."

The "usual tactics" consist of four points: One, ask about something that the interviewee would like to discuss in public. Two, let him talk for as long as possible to make him think that the newspaper is going to give him lots of space. Three, at the end of the interview, when he's convinced he has us nicely under control, ask the one question that really interests us. That way, he'll feel that if he doesn't answer it, we won't give him the space he's hoping for and he will have wasted his time. And four, if he responds evasively, reformulate the question and ask it again. He'll say it's of no interest, but you must get some answer, at least *one* statement. In ninety-nine percent of the cases, the interviewee falls into the trap.

That's all you need. You can throw the rest of the interview away and use that one statement in an article that isn't about the interviewee, but instead about an important subject featuring journalistic research, official facts, unofficial facts, anonymous sources, et cetera.

"If he proves reluctant, tell him we're on his side. You know how journalism works. And it will be to your advantage, too . . ."

Yes, I know how it works. The career of a journalist is as short as an athlete's. We achieve power and glory early, then step aside for the next generation. Very few continue and progress. Most see their standard of living drop and become critics of the press, writing blogs, giving talks, and spending more time than necessary trying to impress their friends. There is no intermediate stage.

I'm still in the category of "promising professional." If I can get those statements, it's likely that next year I won't have to hear someone say "We've got to cut costs" and "With your talent and your name, you won't have any trouble finding another job."

And if I'm promoted? I'll be able to decide what goes on the front page: Should it be the problem of the sheep-eating wolf, the exodus of foreign bankers to Dubai and Singapore, or the ridiculous lack of properties for rent? What a thrilling way to spend the next five years . . .

I go back to my desk, make a few unimportant phone calls, and read everything of interest on various websites. My colleagues are doing the same thing, desperate to find some bit of news that will stop our plummeting sales figures. Someone says that wild boar have been found on the railway line linking Geneva and Zurich. Can I get an article out of that?

Of course. Just as I can out of the phone call I receive from an eighty-year-old woman protesting about the law banning smoking in bars. She says that in summer it's no problem, but in winter we'll have more people dying of pneumonia than of lung cancer because smokers will all be obliged to smoke outside.

What am I doing working at this newspaper?

I know: we love our work and we want to save the world.

SITTING in the lotus position, with incense burning and elevator music playing, I begin my "meditation." People have been advising me to try it for ages. That was when they thought I was just "stressed." (I *was* stressed, but at least that was better than feeling completely indifferent about life.)

"Thoughts will come into your mind. Don't worry. Accept those thoughts, don't try to get rid of them."

Perfect, that's what I'm doing. I drive away toxic emotions like pride, disillusion, jealousy, ingratitude, futility. I fill that space with humility, gratitude, understanding, consciousness, and grace.

I think I've been eating too much sugar, which is bad for your health and for the spiritual body.

I leave aside darkness and despair and invoke the forces of good and of light.

I remember every detail of my lunch with Jacob.

I chant a mantra along with the other pupils.

I wonder if my boss is right. Is Jacob being unfaithful to his wife? Is he being blackmailed?

The teacher asks us to imagine ourselves surrounded by an armor made of light.

"We should live each and every day with the certainty that this armor will protect us from danger, and then we will no longer be bound to the duality of existence. We have to find a middle path, where there is neither joy nor suffering, only profound peace."

I'm beginning to understand why I keep skipping my yoga classes. Duality of existence? A middle path? That sounds as unnatural as keeping my cholesterol level at seventy like my doctor is always telling me I should.

The image of the armor lasts only a few seconds before it's shattered into a thousand pieces and replaced by the absolute certainty that Jacob likes any pretty woman who comes anywhere near him. So why am I bothering with him at all?

The exercises continue. We change posture, and the teacher insists, as she does during every class, that we should try, at least for a few seconds, to "empty our minds."

Emptiness is precisely the thing I fear most and the thing that troubles me most. If she knew what she was asking . . . But then who am I to judge a technique that has lasted for centuries?

What am I doing here?

I know: "De-stressing."

I WAKE up again in the middle of the night. I go to the children's bedrooms to see if everything is all right—it's a bit obsessive, but surely something all parents do now and then.

I go back to bed and lie staring up at the ceiling.

I don't have the strength to say what I do or don't want to do. Why don't I just give up yoga once and for all? Why don't I go to a psychiatrist and start taking those magic pills? Why can't I control myself and stop thinking about Jacob? After all, he never suggested he wanted anything more than someone to talk to about Saturn and the frustrations that all adults face sooner or later.

I can't stand myself any longer. My life is like a film endlessly repeating the same scene.

I took a few classes in psychology when I was studying journalism. In one of them, the professor—a very interesting man, both in class and in bed—said that all interviewees go through five stages: defensiveness, self-promotion, self-confidence, confession, and an attempt to put things right.

In my life, I've gone straight from self-confidence to confession. I'm starting to confess things to myself that would be best left unspoken.

For example: the world has stopped.

Not just my world, but the world of everyone around me. When we meet with friends, we always talk about the same things and the same people. The conversations seem new, but it's all just a waste of time and energy. We're trying to prove that life is still interesting.

Everyone is trying to control their own unhappiness. Not

just Jacob and me, but probably my husband, too. Only he doesn't show it.

In my dangerous confessional state, these things are beginning to become much clearer. I don't feel alone. I'm surrounded by people with the same problems, all of whom are pretending that life is going on as normal. Me. My neighbor. Probably even my boss, as well, and the man sleeping by my side.

After a certain age, we put on a mask of confidence and certainty. In time, that mask gets stuck to our face and we can't remove it.

As children, we learn that if we cry we'll receive affection, that if we show we're sad, we'll be consoled. If we can't get what we want with a smile, then we can surely do so with our tears.

But we no longer cry, except in the bathroom when no one is listening. Nor do we smile at anyone other than our children. We don't show our feelings because people might think we're vulnerable and take advantage of us.

Sleep is the best remedy.

I MEET Jacob as arranged. This time, I choose the place, and we end up in the lovely but neglected Parc des Eaux-Vives, where there's another awful restaurant owned by the city. I once had lunch there with a correspondent from the *Financial Times.* We ordered martinis and the waiter served us Cinzanos.

This time, we don't have lunch in the restaurant, we just sit on the grass and eat sandwiches. He can smoke freely here, because we have a private view of everything around us. We can watch the people coming and going.

I've decided to be honest: after the usual formalities (the weather, work, a "how was the nightclub?"/"I'm going tonight" exchange), the first thing I ask is whether he's being blackmailed because of, how shall I say, an extramarital relationship.

He doesn't seem surprised. He merely asks if I'm speaking as a journalist or as a friend.

At the moment, as a journalist. If you say it's true, I give you my word that the newspaper will support you. We won't publish anything about your personal life, but we will go after the blackmailers.

"Yes, I had an affair with the wife of a friend, which I imagine you already know. He was the one who encouraged it, because we were both bored with our marriages. Do you understand what I'm saying?"

The husband encouraged it? No, I don't understand, but I nod and remember what happened three nights ago, when I had multiple orgasms.

And is the affair still ongoing?

"No, we lost interest. My wife knows about it. There are some things you can't hide. Some people in Nigeria photographed us together and are threatening to publish the pictures, but that's not news to anyone."

Nigeria is where that metallurgical company is based. Didn't his wife threaten divorce?

"She was pretty annoyed for a few days, but no more than that. She has great plans for our marriage, and I imagine that fidelity isn't necessarily part of them. She pretended to be a bit jealous, just to show that what happened was important, but she's a terrible actress. A few hours after I'd confessed, her mind was already on other things."

It would seem that Jacob lives in a completely different world from mine, where wives don't feel jealous and husbands encourage their wives to have affairs. Am I missing out?

"Time heals everything, don't you think?"

That depends. Time can often make things worse. That's what's happening with me, but I came here to interview, not to be interviewed, so I don't say anything. He goes on:

"The Nigerians don't know this. I've set a trap for them with the Ministry of Finance and arranged to record everything, exactly as they did with me."

At that point, I see my article go out the window, and along with it my big chance of rising up the ladder in a dying industry. There's nothing new to be told—no adultery, no blackmail, no corruption. Everything is following the Swiss pattern of quality and excellence.

"Have you finished asking questions? Can we move on to another subject?"

Yes, I've asked all my questions, but I don't really have another subject.

"I think you should have asked why I wanted to see you again. And why I wanted to know if you were happy. Do you think I'm interested in you sexually? We're not teenagers anymore. I confess that I was surprised by what you did in my office, and I loved coming in your mouth, but that isn't enough of a reason for why we are here, especially considering we can't do that kind of thing in a public place. So don't you want to know why I wanted to meet you again?"

The jack-in-the-box of that question about whether or not I'm happy springs out at me again. Doesn't he realize that you don't ask that kind of thing?

Only if you want to tell me, I reply, in order to provoke him and destroy, once and for all, that arrogant air of his that makes me feel so insecure. Then I add: It's because you want to go to bed with me. You won't be the first I've told "no."

He shakes his head. I pretend to be unfazed and point at the waves on the normally calm surface of the lake below. We sit looking at them as if they were the most interesting thing in the world until he manages to find the right words:

"As you no doubt realized, I asked if you were happy because I recognized myself in you. Similarities attract. You may not feel the same about me, but that doesn't matter. You may be mentally exhausted, convinced that your nonexistent problems—problems you know are nonexistent—are draining you of all your energy.'

I had that exact thought during lunch; tortured souls recognize each other and are drawn together in order to frighten the living.

"I feel the same," he says. "Except that my problems are more real. Since I depend on the approval of so many people, I am filled with self-loathing when I haven't resolved this or that problem. And that makes me feel useless. I've thought of seeking medical help, but my wife doesn't want me to. She says that if anyone found out, it could ruin my career. I agree."

So he talks about these things with his wife. Perhaps

tonight I'll do the same with my husband. Instead of going to a nightclub, I could sit down with him and tell him everything. How would he react?

"Of course, I've made a lot of mistakes," he continues. "At the moment I'm trying to force myself to look at the world differently, but it's not working. When I see someone like you—and I've met a lot of people in the same situation—I try to find out how they're dealing with the problem. I need help, you see, and that's the only way I can get it."

So that's it. No sex, no great romantic affair to bring a little sunshine into the gray Geneva afternoon. He just wants a support group, the kind of thing alcoholics and drug addicts have.

I get up.

I look him straight in the eye and say that I'm actually very happy, and that he should go to a psychiatrist. His wife can't control everything in his life. Besides, medical confidentiality would guarantee that no one would find out. I have a friend who was cured by taking pills. Does he want to spend the rest of his life haunted by the specter of depression just to be reelected? Is that what he wants for his future?

He looks around to see if anyone is listening. I've already done that, and I know we're alone apart from a group of drug dealers on the other side of the park, behind the restaurant. But they won't bother us.

I can't stop. The more I talk, the more I realize that I'm hearing myself and it's helping. I say that negativity feeds on itself. He needs to look for something that will give him a little joy, like sailing, or going to the movies, or reading.

"No, that's not it. You don't understand." He seems startled by my response.

I do understand. Every day we're bombarded with information and images—with adolescents in heavy makeup pretending to be grown women as they advertise miraculous creams promising eternal beauty; with the story of an aging couple who climbed Mount Everest to celebrate their wedding anniversary; with new massage gizmos, and pharmacy windows that are chockablock with slimming products; with movies that give an entirely false impression of reality, and books promising fantastic results; with specialists who give advice about how to succeed in life or find inner peace. And all these things make us feel old, make us feel that we're leading dull, unadventurous lives as our skin grows ever more flaccid, and the pounds pile on irrevocably. And yet we feel obliged to repress our emotions and our desires, because they don't fit with what we call "maturity."

Choose what information you listen to. Place a filter over your eyes and ears and allow in only things that won't bring you down, because we have our day-to-day life to do that. Do you think I don't get judged and criticized at work? Well, I do—a lot! But I've decided to hear only the things that encourage me to improve, the things that help me correct my mistakes. Otherwise, I will just pretend I can't hear the other stuff or block it out.

I came here in search of a complicated story involving adultery, blackmail, and corruption. But you've dealt with it all in the best possible way. Can't you see that?

Without thinking, I sit down again and grasp his head so that he can't escape. I give him a long kiss. He hesitates for a fraction of a second, then responds. Immediately, all my feelings of impotence, fragility, failure, and insecurity are replaced by one of immense euphoria. From one moment to the next, I have suddenly become wise, I have regained control of the situation and dared to do something that before I could only imagine. I have ventured into unknown territory and dangerous waters, destroying pyramids and building sanctuaries.

I am once again the mistress of my thoughts and my actions.

What seemed impossible this morning has become reality this afternoon. I can feel again, and I can love something I don't possess. The wind has ceased to bother me and has become instead a blessing, like the caress of a god on my cheek. I have my soul back.

Hundreds of years seem to pass during the short time the kiss lasts. We separate slowly, and, as he gently strokes my hair, we look deep into each other's eyes.

And we find exactly what was there before.

Sadness.

Now with the addition of a stupid, irresponsible gesture that, at least in my case, will only make matters worse.

We spend another half an hour together, talking about the city and its inhabitants as if nothing had happened. We seemed very close when we arrived at the park, and we became one when we kissed. Now, however, we are two complete strangers, trying to keep the conversation going just long enough so that we can each go our separate ways without too much embarrassment.

No one saw us—we're not in a restaurant. Our marriages are safe.

I consider apologizing, but know it's not necessary. After all, it was only a kiss.

I CAN'T honestly say that I feel victorious, but at least I've recovered some self-control. At home, everything carries on as usual; before I was in a terrible state, and now I'm feeling better. No one asks me how I am.

I'm going to follow Jacob König's example and talk to my husband about my strange state of mind. I'll confide in him, and I'm sure he'll be able to help me.

On the other hand, I feel so good today; why spoil it by confessing to things I don't even understand myself? I continue to struggle. I don't believe that what I'm going through can be put down to a lack of chemical elements in my body, as I've read online about "compulsive sadness."

I'm not sad today. It's just one of those phases we all go through. I remember when my high-school class organized its farewell party; we laughed for two hours and then, at the end, we all sobbed because we knew we were parting forever. The sadness lasted for a few days or weeks, I can't quite remember. But the mere fact that I don't remember says something very important: it's over. Turning thirty was hard, and perhaps I just wasn't ready for it.

My husband goes upstairs to put the children to bed. I pour myself a glass of wine and go out into the garden.

It's still windy. It's a wind we know well here; it can blow for three, six, or even nine days. In France—a more romantic country than Switzerland—it's known as the mistral and it always brings bright, cold weather. It's high time these clouds went away. Tomorrow it will be sunny.

I keep thinking about the conversation in the park, that kiss. I feel no regrets at all. I did something I'd never done before, and that in itself has begun to break down the walls imprisoning me.

It doesn't really matter what Jacob König thinks. I can't spend my life trying to please other people.

I finish my glass of wine and refill it, and for the first time in many months, I feel something other than apathy or a sense of futility.

My husband comes downstairs dressed for a party and asks how long it will take me to get ready. I'd forgotten that we'd agreed to go dancing tonight.

I race upstairs, and when I come back down, I see that our Filipino babysitter has arrived and has already spread her books across the living-room table. The children are in bed asleep and shouldn't be any trouble, and so she uses her time to study. She seems to have an aversion to television.

We're ready to leave. I've put on my best dress, even at the risk of dressing to the nines for a laid-back party. What does it matter? I need to celebrate.

I WAKE to the sound of the wind rattling the windows. I blame my husband for not shutting them properly. I feel the need to get up and perform my nightly ritual of going into the children's bedrooms to check that everything's all right. And yet something stops me. Is it because I had too much to drink? I start to think about the waves I saw earlier at the lake, about the clouds that have now dissipated and the person who was with me. I remember very little about the nightclub; we both thought the music was horrible and the atmosphere extremely dull. It wasn't long before we were back at our respective computers.

What about all those things I said to Jacob this afternoon? Shouldn't I take a little time to think about them myself?

This room is suffocating me. My perfect husband is asleep beside me; he doesn't seem to have heard the wind rattling the windows. I imagine Jacob lying beside his wife and telling her everything he feels (although I'm sure he won't say anything about me). He's relieved to have someone who can help him when he feels most alone. I don't really believe what he said about her—if it were true, they would have separated. After all, they don't have any children to worry about!

I wonder if the mistral has woken him up, too, and what he and his wife will talk about now. Where do they live? It wouldn't be hard to find out. I can find out when I get in to work tomorrow. I wonder: Did they make love tonight? Did he take her passionately, did she moan with pleasure?

The way I behave with him is always a surprise. Oral sex, sensible advice, that kiss in the park. I seem like another person. Who is this woman I become whenever I'm with Jacob?

My provocative adolescent self. The one who was once as

steady as a rock and as strong as the wind ruffling the calm waters of Lake Léman. It's odd how whenever we meet up with old school friends, we always think they haven't changed at all, even if the weakest has grown strong, the prettiest has ended up with a monster for a husband, and those who seemed closest have grown apart and not seen one another for years.

With Jacob, though, at least in the early stages of this reunion, I can still go back in time and be the young girl who isn't afraid of consequences. She's only sixteen, and the return of Saturn, which will bring maturity, is still a long way off.

I try to sleep, but I can't. I spend an hour thinking about him obsessively. I remember my next-door neighbor washing his car and how I judged his life to be "pointless," occupied by useless things. It's not useless: he probably enjoys himself, taking the opportunity to get some exercise and see life's simple things as blessings, not curses.

That's what I need to do: relax a little and enjoy life more. I can't keep thinking about Jacob. I am replacing my missing joy with something more concrete—a man—but that's not the point. If I went to a psychiatrist, he'd tell me that this isn't my problem at all; instead, it's a lack of lithium, low levels of serotonin, and so on. This didn't begin with Jacob's appearance on the scene, and it won't end with his departure.

But I can't forget him. My mind repeats the moment of that kiss over and over.

And I realize that my unconscious is transforming an imaginary problem into a real one. That's what always happens. That's how illnesses come about.

I never want to see that man again. He's been sent by the devil to destabilize something that was already fragile. How could I fall in love so quickly with someone I don't even know? And who says I'm in love? I've been having problems since the spring. If things were perfectly fine before that, I see no reason why they shouldn't be again.

I repeat what I said before: It's just a phase.

I need to stay focused and hold negativity at bay. Wasn't that my advice to Jacob?

I must stand firm and wait for the crisis to pass. Otherwise, I run the risk of really falling in love, and of feeling permanently what I felt for only a fraction of a second when we had lunch together that first time. And if that happens, things won't just happen inside me. No, the suffering and pain will spread everywhere.

I lie tossing and turning in bed for what feels like ages before I fall asleep. After what seems only a second, my husband wakes me up. It's a bright day, the sky is blue, and the mistral is still blowing.

IT'S breakfast time," my husband says. "I'd better go and get the kids up."

Why don't we swap roles for once? I suggest. You go to the kitchen and I'll get the kids ready for school.

"Is that a challenge?" he asks. "If it is, you're going to have the best breakfast you've had in years."

No, it isn't a challenge, I just want to change things around a bit. So, you don't think the breakfast I make is good enough?

"Listen, it's far too early for arguments. Last night we both had a bit too much to drink, and nightclubs really aren't meant for people our age," he says. "Anyway, okay, you go and get the children ready."

He leaves before I can respond. I pick up my smartphone and check what things I have to do today.

I look down the list of commitments that can't be put off. The longer the list, the more productive I consider my day to be. Many of the tasks are things I promised to do the day before or during the week, but which I haven't yet done. That's why the list keeps growing, until it makes me so nervous that I decide to scrap the whole thing and start again. And then I realize that nothing on the list is actually very important.

There's something that isn't on the list, though, something I'm definitely not going to forget: finding out where Jacob König lives and taking a moment to drive past his house.

When I go downstairs, the table is perfectly set with fruit salad, olive oil, cheese, whole-grain bread, yogurt, and plums. A copy of the newspaper I work for is placed discreetly to the left. My husband has long since given up reading print media and is consulting his iPad. Our oldest son asks what "blackmail" means. I can't understand why he wants to know until I see the front page. There is a large photo of Jacob, one of many he must have sent to the press. He looks thoughtful, reflective. Next to the photo is the headline: "Deputy Reports Blackmail Attempt."

I didn't write the article. In fact, while I was at my meeting with Jacob, the editor-in-chief rang to say that I could cancel because they had received a communiqué from the Ministry of Finance and were working on the case. I explained that the meeting had already taken place, that it had happened more quickly than I'd expected and without any need for the "usual tactics." I was then dispatched to a nearby neighborhood (which considers itself a "city" and even has a prefecture) whose grocery store was caught selling food that's past its sell-by date. I talked to the owner of the store, to neighbors and friends of neighbors, something I'm sure our readers found made for a more interesting article than some political scandal. It also made the front page, but without the banner headlines. "Grocery Store Fined, No Reports of Food Poisoning."

Seeing that photo of Jacob right there on our breakfast table troubles me deeply.

I tell my husband that we need to have a talk—tonight.

"We can leave the children with my mother and go to dinner somewhere, just the two of us," he says. "I need to spend a bit of time with you as well, alone and without any terrible music blaring in our ears. How can people possibly like that?"

IT WAS a spring morning.

I was sitting in a corner of the playground that was usually deserted and studying the tiles on the school wall. I knew there was something wrong with me.

The other children all thought I acted "better than them," and I never made any attempt to deny this. On the contrary. I made my mother keep buying me expensive clothes and taking me to school in her pricey foreign car.

But that day in the playground, I realized that I was alone, and might remain alone for the rest of my life. Even though I was only eight years old, it seemed like it was already too late to change and to prove to the other children that I was just like them.

Now, summer.

I was at secondary school, and the boys were always hitting on me, no matter how hard I tried to fend them off. The other girls were green with envy, but pretended not to be and were always hanging around and cozying up to me, hoping to pick up any rejects.

And I rejected almost everyone, because I knew that if anyone ever managed to enter my world, they would find nothing of interest. It was best to maintain an air of mystery with a hint of unattainable pleasures.

On my way home, I noticed a few mushrooms that had sprung up after the rain. They were perfect and intact because everyone knew they were poisonous. For a fraction of a second, I considered eating them. I wasn't feeling particularly sad or particularly happy; I just wanted to get my parents' attention.

I didn't eat the mushrooms.

Now it's the first day of autumn, the loveliest season of the year. Soon the leaves will change color and each tree will be different from all the others. On the way to the car park, I decide to take a slightly different route.

I stop in front of the school where I studied. The tile wall is still there. Nothing has changed, except for the fact that I'm no longer alone. In my mind are two men; one will never be mine, but I'll have dinner tonight with the other one in some special, carefully chosen spot.

A bird flies across the sky, playing with the wind. It flies back and forth, rises and falls, its movements obeying some logic I cannot understand. Perhaps the only logic is that of having fun.

I am not a bird. I can't spend my life playing like many of our friends, who have less money but who seem to spend their whole lives traveling or going to restaurants. I've tried to be like that, but I can't. Thanks to my husband's influence, I got the job I have now. I work, I fill my time, I feel useful and able to justify my existence. One day, my children will be proud of their mother, and my childhood friends will be more frustrated than ever, because I have managed to build something tangible while they have devoted themselves to looking after the house, the children, and their husband.

Perhaps they don't have this need to impress other people. I do, and I can't reject it, because it's been a good influence on my life, driving me on. As long as I don't take any unnecessary risks, of course. As long as I manage to preserve my world exactly as it is today.

As soon as I get to the office, I search through the government's digital archives. It takes me less than a minute to find Jacob König's address, as well as information about how much he earns, where he studied, the name of his wife, and where she works.

MY HUSBAND has chosen a restaurant halfway between my office and our house. We've been there before. I like the food, the wine, and the atmosphere, but I always feel that we eat better at home. I dine out only when my social life requires it, and, whenever I can, I avoid it. I love cooking. I love being with my family, feeling that I'm both protector and protected.

One of the tasks not on my to-do list this morning was "drive past Jacob König's house." I managed to resist the impulse. I have enough imaginary problems without adding the real problem of unrequited love. The feelings I had are long over. It won't happen again. We can now proceed into a future of peace, hope, and prosperity.

"They say the owner has changed and the food isn't quite as good," says my husband.

It doesn't matter. Restaurant food is always the same: too much butter, ostentatious presentation, and—because we live in one of the most expensive cities in the world—an exorbitant price for something that really isn't worth it.

But eating out is a ritual. We are greeted by the headwaiter, who leads us to our usual table even though we haven't been here for some time. He asks if we want the same wine (of course we do) and hands us the menu. I read it from beginning to end and choose the same thing as always. My husband opts for his traditional choice, roast lamb with lentils. The waiter comes to tell us about today's chef's specials: we listen politely, grunt appreciatively, then order.

———

The first glass of wine doesn't need to be tasted and meticulously analyzed because we've been married for ten years. It goes down very quickly, among talk of work and complaints about the man who was supposed to come and fix the central heating but never turned up.

"And how are you getting on with that article about next Sunday's elections?" my husband asks.

I've been commissioned to write about a question I find particularly interesting: Does the electorate have a right to scrutinize a politician's private life? It's a response to the news that a deputy is being blackmailed by Nigerians. Most of the people I interviewed said they don't care. It's not like it is in the United States, they say, and we're proud of that.

We talk about other recent news items. The increase in the number of voters at the last election for the Council of States. The drivers working for Geneva's public transport company, TPG, who are tired but happy with their work. A woman who was run over in a crosswalk. The train that broke down and blocked the line for more than two hours. And other such pointless topics.

I pour myself another glass of wine, without waiting for the appetizer and without asking my husband what his day was like. He listens politely to everything I've just said. He must be wondering what we're doing here.

"You seem happier today," he says after the waiter has brought our main course, and after I realize I've been talking nonstop for twenty minutes. "Has something special happened to cheer you up?"

If he'd asked that same question on the day I went to Parc des Eaux-Vives, I would have blushed and immediately come out with the string of excuses I'd saved up. But today has been another normal, tedious day despite my attempts to convince myself that I'm very important to the world.

"What was it you wanted to talk to me about?"

I take a sip from my third glass of wine and prepare to make a full confession. The waiter arrives and stops me just as I'm about to leap into the abyss. We exchange a few more meaningless words, wasting precious minutes of my life on pointless niceties.

My husband orders another bottle of wine. The waiter wishes us "bon appétit" and goes off to fetch the new bottle. Then I begin.

You'll say that I need to see a doctor, but I don't. I cope perfectly well with my work at home and in the office, but for some months now I've been feeling sad.

"You could have fooled me. Like I just said, you seem much happier."

Of course. My sadness has become so routine that no one notices anymore. It's really good to finally talk about it, but what I have to say runs deeper than that false happiness. I don't sleep properly anymore. I feel I'm just being self-obsessed, trying to impress people as if I were a child. I cry alone in the shower for no reason. I've only really enjoyed making love once in many months, and you know what time I'm talking about. I thought perhaps I was going through a midlife crisis, but that isn't enough of an explanation. I feel like I'm wasting my life, that one day I'll look back and regret everything I've done, apart from having married you and having our lovely children.

"But isn't that what matters most?"

For lots of people, yes. But it isn't enough for me. It's getting worse every day. When I finally finish my housework each evening, an endless dialogue starts in my head. I'm afraid of things changing, but at the same time I'm dying to experience something different. My thoughts keep repeating themselves uncontrollably. You don't notice because you're asleep.

For example, did you notice the mistral last night rattling the windows?

"No, the windows were shut."

That's what I mean. Even a high wind that has blown thousands of times since we've been married is capable of waking me up. I notice when you turn over in bed and when you talk in your sleep. But please don't take this personally—it seems like I'm surrounded by things that make no sense. Just to be clear, though: I love our children. I love you. I adore my work. But that only makes me feel worse, because I feel I'm being unfair to God, to life, to you.

He's barely touched his food. It's as if he were sitting opposite a complete stranger. But saying these words has already filled me with an enormous peace. My secret is out. The wine is having its effect. I am no longer alone. Thank you, Jacob König.

"Do you think you need to see a doctor?"

I don't know. Even if I did, I don't want to go down that road. I need to learn how to resolve my problems on my own.

"It must have been very difficult to keep all these emotions to yourself for so long. Thank you for telling me. But why didn't you tell me before?"

Because it's only now that things have become unbearable. I was thinking today about my childhood and teenage years. Does the root of all this lie there? I don't think so, not unless my mind has been lying to me all these years, which I think is unlikely. I come from a normal family, I had a normal upbringing, I lead a normal life. What's wrong with me?

I didn't say anything before—I tell him, crying now—because I thought it would pass and I didn't want to worry you.

"You're definitely not crazy. I haven't noticed any of this. You haven't been particularly irritable, you haven't lost weight, and if you can control your feelings that well, then there must be a way out of this."

Why did he mention losing weight?

"I can ask our doctor to prescribe some tranquilizers to help you sleep. I'll say they're for me. I think that if you could sleep properly, then you would gradually regain control of your thoughts. Perhaps we should exercise more. The children would love it. We're far too caught up in work, and that's not good."

I'm not that caught up in my work. Despite what you think, the idiotic articles I write help me keep my mind occupied and drive away the wild thoughts that overwhelm me as soon as I have nothing to do.

"But we do need more exercise, more time outdoors. To run until we drop with exhaustion. And perhaps we should invite friends round more often."

That would be a complete nightmare! Having to talk and entertain people with a fixed smile on my lips, listening to their views on opera and traffic. Then, to top it all, having to clean up afterward.

"Let's go to the Jura National Park this weekend. We haven't been there for ages."

The elections are this weekend. I'll be on duty at the newspaper.

We eat in silence. The waiter has already been to our table twice to see if we've finished, but we haven't even touched our plates. We make short work of the second bottle of wine. I can imagine what my husband's thinking: "How can I help my wife? What can I do to make her happy?" Nothing. Nothing more than he's doing already. I would hate it if he arrived home bearing a box of chocolates or a bouquet of flowers.

We conclude that he's had too much to drink to drive

home, so we'll have to leave the car at the restaurant and fetch it tomorrow. I telephone my mother-in-law and ask if the children can sleep over. I'll be there early tomorrow morning to take them to school.

"But what exactly is missing in your life?"

Please don't ask me that. Because the answer is nothing. Nothing! If only I had some serious problem. I don't know anyone who's going through quite the same thing. Even a friend of mine, who spent years feeling depressed, is now getting treatment. I don't think I need that, because I don't have the symptoms she described. I don't want to enter the dangerous territory of legal drugs. People might be angry, stressed, or grieving over a broken heart—and in the latter case, they might *think* they're depressed and in need of medicines and drugs—but they're not. They're just suffering from a broken heart, and there have been broken hearts ever since the world began, ever since man discovered that mysterious thing called Love.

"If you don't want to go and see a doctor, why don't you do some research?"

I've tried. I've spent ages looking at psychology websites. I've devoted myself more seriously to yoga. Haven't you noticed the books I've been bringing home lately? Did you think I'd suddenly become less literary and more spiritual?

No, I'm looking for an answer I can't find. After reading about ten of those self-help books, I saw that they were leading nowhere. They have an immediate effect, but that effect stops as soon as I close the book. They're just words, describing an ideal world that doesn't exist, not even for the people who wrote them.

"But do you feel better now?"

Of course, but that isn't the problem. I need to know who I've become, because I am that person. It's not something external.

I can see that he's trying desperately to help, but he's as lost as I am. He keeps talking about symptoms, but that, I tell him, isn't the problem. Everything is a symptom. Can you imagine a kind of spongy black hole?

"No."

Well, that's what it is.

He assures me that I will get out of this situation. I mustn't judge myself. I mustn't blame myself. He's on my side.

"There's light at the end of the tunnel."

I'd like to believe you, but it's as if my feet are stuck in concrete. Meanwhile, don't worry, I'll keep fighting. I've been fighting all these months. I've been in similar situations before, and they've always passed. One day I'll wake up and all this will just be a bad dream. I really believe that.

He asks for the bill, he takes my hand, we call a taxi. Something has gotten better. Trusting the one you love always brings good results.

JACOB König, what are you doing in my bedroom, in my bed, and in my nightmares? You should be working. After all, it's only three days until the elections for the Municipal Council and you've already wasted precious hours of your campaign having lunch with me at La Perle du Lac and talking in the Parc des Eaux-Vives.

Isn't that enough? What are you doing in my dreams? I did exactly as you suggested; I talked to my husband, and I felt the love he feels for me. And afterward, when we made love more passionately than we have in a while, the feeling that happiness had been sucked out of my life disappeared completely.

Please go away. Tomorrow's going to be a difficult day. I have to get up early to take the children to school, then go to the store, find somewhere to park, and think up something original to say about a very unoriginal topic—politics. Leave me alone, Jacob König.

I'm happily married. And you don't even know that I'm thinking about you. I wish I had someone here with me tonight to tell me stories with happy endings, to sing a song that would send me to sleep. But no, all I can think of is you.

I'm losing control. It's been a week since I saw you, but you're still here.

If you don't disappear, I'll have to go to your house and have tea with you and your wife, to see with my own eyes how happy you are. To see that I don't stand a chance, that you lied when you said you could see yourself reflected in me, that you consciously allowed me to bring the wound of that unsolicited kiss upon myself.

I hope you understand. I pray that you do, because even I can't understand what it is that I'm asking.

I get up and go over to the computer, intending to Google "How to get your man." Instead, I type in "depression." I need to be absolutely clear about what's happening.

I find a website with a self-diagnosis questionnaire titled "Find Out if You Have a Psychological Problem." My response to most of the questions is "No."

Result: "You're going through a difficult time, but you are definitely not clinically depressed. There's no need to go to a doctor."

Isn't that what I said? I knew it. I'm not ill. I'm just inventing all this to get some attention. Or am I deceiving myself, trying to make my life a little more interesting with *problems*? Problems require solutions and I can spend my hours, my days, my weeks, looking for them. Perhaps it might be a good idea, after all, if my husband asked our doctor to prescribe something to help me sleep. Perhaps it's just the stress of work that's making me so tense, especially since it is election time. I try so hard to be better than the others, both at work and in my personal life, and it's not easy to balance the two.

TODAY is Saturday, the eve of the elections. I have a friend who says he hates weekends because when the stock market is closed he has no way to amuse himself.

My husband has persuaded me that we need to get out of the city. His argument is that the kids will enjoy a little trip, even if we can't go away for the whole weekend because tomorrow I'm working.

He tells me to wear my jogging pants. I feel embarrassed going out like that, especially to visit Nyon, the ancient and glorious city that was once home to the Romans but now has fewer than twenty thousand inhabitants. I tell him that jogging pants are really something you wear closer to home, where it's obvious that you're intending to exercise, but he insists.

I don't want to argue, so I do as he asks. I don't want to argue with anyone about anything—not now. The less said, the better.

While I'm off to a picnic in a small town less than half an hour away, Jacob will be visiting voters, talking to aides and friends, and feeling nervous, perhaps a little stressed, but glad because something is happening in his life. Opinion polls in Switzerland don't count for much, because here secrecy of the vote is taken very seriously; however, it seems likely that he'll be reelected.

His wife must have spent a sleepless night, but for very different reasons from mine. She'll be planning how to receive their friends after the result is officially announced. This morning she'll be at the market in Rue de Rive, where, all week, stalls selling fruit and cheese and meat are set up right outside the Julius Baer Bank and the shop windows of Prada, Gucci,

Armani, and other designer brands. She chooses the best of everything, without worrying about the cost. Then she might take her car and drive to Satigny to visit one of the many vineyards that are the pride of the region, to taste some of the new vintages, and to decide on something that will please those who really understand wine—as seems to be the case with her husband.

She will return home tired, but happy. Officially, Jacob is still campaigning, but why not get things ready for the evening? Oh, dear, now she realizes that she has less cheese than she thought! She gets in the car again and goes back to the market. Among the dozens of varieties on display, she chooses the cheeses that are the pride of the Canton of Vaud: Gruyère (all three varieties: mild, *salé,* and the most expensive of all, which takes nine to twelve months to mature), Tomme Vaudoise (soft and creamy, to be eaten in a fondue or on its own), and L'Etivaz (made from the milk of cows grazed in alpine pastures and prepared in the traditional way, in copper cauldrons, over open wood fires).

Is it worth popping in to one of the shops and buying something new to wear? Or would that appear ostentatious? Best to wear that Moschino outfit she bought in Milan when she accompanied her husband to a conference on labor laws.

And how will Jacob be feeling?

He phones his wife every hour to ask if he should say this or that, if it would be best to visit this street or that area, or if the *Tribune de Genève* has posted anything new on its website. He depends on her and her advice, offloads some of the tension that builds up with each visit he makes, and asks her about the strategy they drew up together and where he should go next. As he suggested during our conversation in the park, the only reason he stays in politics is so he doesn't disappoint her. Even though he hates what he's doing, love lends a unique quality to his efforts. If he continues on his brilliant path, he will one day be president of the republic. Admittedly, this doesn't mean very much in Switzerland, because as we all know, the president changes every year and is elected by the Federal Council. But who wouldn't like to say that her husband was president of Switzerland, otherwise known as the Swiss Confederation?

It will open doors, bring invitations to conferences in far-flung places. Some large company will appoint him to its board. The future of the Königs looks bright, while all that lies before me at this precise moment is the road and the prospect of a picnic while wearing a hideous pair of jogging pants.

THE FIRST thing we do is visit the Roman museum and then climb a small hill to see some ruins. Our children race around, laughing. Now that my husband knows everything, I feel relieved. I don't need to pretend all the time.

"Let's go and run round the lake."

What about the kids?

My husband spots a couple family friends sitting on a nearby bench, eating ice cream with their children. "Should we ask them if our kids can join? We can buy them ice cream, too."

Our friends are surprised to see us, but agree. Before we go down to the shore of Lake Léman—which all foreigners call Lake Geneva—he buys the ice cream for the children and asks them to stay with our friends while Mommy and Daddy go for a run. My son complains that he hasn't got his iPad. My husband goes to the car and fetches the stupid thing. From that moment on, the screen will be the best possible nanny. They won't budge until they've killed terrorists in games more suited to adults.

We start running. On one side are gardens; on the other, seagulls and sailboats making the most of the mistral. The wind didn't stop on the third day, nor on the sixth. It must be nearing its ninth day, when it will disappear and take with it the blue sky and the good weather. We run along the track for fifteen minutes. We've left Nyon behind us and had better head back.

I haven't exercised in ages. When we've been running for twenty minutes, I stop. I can't go on. I'll have to walk the rest of the way.

"Of course you can do it!" encourages my husband, jogging in place so as not to lose his rhythm. "Don't stop, keep running."

I bend forward, resting my hands on my knees. My heart is pounding; it's the fault of all those sleepless nights. He keeps jogging circles round me.

"Come on, you can do it! It's worse if you stop. Do it for me, for the kids. This isn't just a way of getting some exercise, it's reminding you that there's a finish line and that you can't give up halfway through."

Is he talking about my "compulsive sadness"?

He stops jogging, takes my hands, and gently shakes me. I'm too tired to run, but I'm too tired to resist as well. I do as he asks. We run together for the remaining ten minutes.

I pass billboards for the various Council of States candidates, which I hadn't noticed before. Among the photos is one of Jacob König, smiling at the camera.

I run more quickly. My husband is surprised and speeds up. We get there in seven minutes instead of ten. The children haven't moved. Despite the beautiful surroundings—the mountains, the seagulls, the Alps in the distance—they have their eyes glued to the screen of that soul-sucking machine.

My husband goes to them, but I keep running. He watches me, surprised and happy. He must think his words have had an effect and are filling my body with the endorphins that fill our blood whenever we do some physical activity with a slight intensity, like when we run or have an orgasm. The hormones' main effects are improving our mood, boosting our immune system, and fending off premature aging, but, above all, they provoke a feeling of euphoria and pleasure.

However, that isn't what the endorphins are doing for me. They're merely giving me the strength to carry on, to run as far as the horizon and leave everything behind. Why do I have to have such wonderful children? Why did I have to meet my husband and fall in love? If I hadn't met him, I'd be a free woman now.

I'm mad. I should run straight to the nearest mental hospital, because these are not the kinds of things one should think. But I continue to think them.

I run for a few more minutes, then go back. Halfway, I'm terrified by the possibility that my wish for freedom will come true and I'll find no one there when I go back to the park in Nyon.

But there they are, smiling at their loving mother and spouse. I embrace them all. I'm sweating, my body and mind dirty, but still I hold them close.

Despite what I feel. Or, rather, despite what I don't feel.

YOU don't choose your life; it chooses you. There's no point asking why life has reserved certain joys or griefs, you just accept them and carry on.

We can't choose our lives, but we can decide what to do with the joys or griefs we're given.

That Sunday afternoon, I'm at the party headquarters doing my professional duty. I managed to convince my boss of this, and now I'm trying to convince myself. It's a quarter to six and people are celebrating. Contrary to my fevered imaginings, none of the elected candidates will be holding a reception, and so I still won't get a chance to go to the house of Jacob and Marianne König.

When I arrive, the first results are just coming in. More than forty-five percent of the electorate voted, which is a record. A female candidate came out on top, and Jacob came in an honorable third, which will give him the right to enter government if his party chooses him.

The main hall is decorated with yellow and green balloons. People have already started to drink, and some make the victory sign, perhaps hoping that tomorrow their picture will appear in the newspaper. But the photographers haven't yet arrived; after all, it's Sunday, and the weather is lovely.

Jacob spots me at once and immediately looks the other way, searching for someone with whom he can talk about matters that must, I imagine, be extraordinarily dull.

I need to work, or at least pretend to. I take out my digital recorder, a notebook, and a felt-tip pen. I walk back and forth, collecting statements such as "Now we can get that law on immigration through" or "The voters realize that they made the wrong choice last time and now they've voted me back in."

The winner says: "It was the female vote that really counted for me."

Léman Bleu, the local television station, has set up a studio in the main room, and its female political presenter—a vague object of desire for nine out of ten men there—is asking intelligent questions but receiving only the sound bites approved by the political aides.

At one point, Jacob König is called for an interview, and I try to get closer to hear what he's saying. Someone blocks my path.

"Hello, I'm Madame König. Jacob has told me a lot about you."

What a woman! Blond, blue-eyed, and wearing an elegant black cardigan with a red Hermès scarf, although that's the only famous brand name I can spot. Her other clothes must have been made exclusively by the best couturier in Paris, whose name must be kept secret in order to avoid copycat designs.

I try not to look surprised.

Jacob told you about me? I did interview him, and, a few days later, we had lunch together. I know journalists aren't supposed to have an opinion about their interviewees, but I think your husband is a brave man to have gone public about that blackmail attempt.

Marianne—or Mme König, as she introduced herself—pretends to be interested in what I'm saying. She must know more than she is letting on. Would Jacob have told her what happened during our meeting in the Parc des Eaux-Vives? Should I mention it?

The interview with Léman Bleu has just begun, but she doesn't seem to be interested in listening to what her husband says. She probably knows it all by heart, anyway. She doubtless chose his pale blue shirt and gray tie, his beautifully cut flannel jacket, and the watch he's wearing—not too expensive, to avoid appearing ostentatious, but not too cheap, either, to show a proper respect for one of the country's main industries.

I ask if she has anything to say. She replies that as an assistant professor of philosophy at the University of Geneva, she would be delighted to comment, but as the wife of a reelected politician, that would be absurd.

It seems to me that she's provoking me, and so I decide to pay her back in kind.

I say I admire her dignity. She knew her husband had had an affair with the wife of a friend and yet she didn't create a scandal. Not even when it appeared in the newspapers just before the elections.

"Of course not. When it's a matter of consensual sex without love, I'm in favor of open relationships."

Is she insinuating something? I can't quite look into the blue beacons that are her eyes. I notice only that she doesn't wear much makeup. She doesn't need to.

"In fact," she says, "it was my idea to get an anonymous informer to tell the newspaper the week before the elections. People will soon forget a marital infidelity, but they'll always remember his bravery at denouncing corruption even though it could have had serious repercussions for his family life."

She laughs at that last bit and tells me that what she's saying is strictly off the record, of course, and should not be published.

I say that according to the rules of journalism, people should request that something be kept off the record *before* they speak. The journalist can then agree or not. Asking afterward is like trying to stop a leaf that has fallen into the river and is already traveling wherever the waters choose to take it. The leaf can no longer make its own decisions.

"But you won't repeat it, will you? I'm sure you don't have the slightest interest in damaging my husband's reputation."

In less than five minutes of conversation, there is already evident hostility between us. Feeling embarrassed, I agree to treat her statement as off the record. She notes that on any similar occasion, she will ask first. She learns something new every minute. She gets closer and closer to her ambition every minute. Yes, *her* ambition, because Jacob said that he was unhappy with the life he leads.

She doesn't take her eyes off me. I decide to resume my role as journalist and ask if she has anything more to add. Has she organized a party at home for close friends?

"Of course not! Imagine how much work that would be. Besides, he's already been elected. You hold any parties and dinners before an election, to draw votes."

Again, I feel like a complete imbecile, but I need to ask at least one other question.

Is Jacob happy?

And I see that I have hit home. Mme König gives me a condescending look and replies slowly, as if she were a teacher giving me a lesson:

"Of course he's happy. Why on earth wouldn't he be?"

This woman deserves to be drawn and quartered.

We are both interrupted at the same time—me by an aide wanting to introduce me to the winner, she by an acquaintance coming to offer his congratulations. It was a pleasure to meet her, I say, and am tempted to add that, on another occasion, I'd like to explore what she means by consensual sex with the wife of a friend—off the record, of course—but there's no time. I give her my card should she ever need to contact me, but she does not reciprocate. Before I move away, however, she grabs my arm and, in front of the aide and the man who has come to congratulate her on her husband's victory, says:

"I saw that mutual friend of ours who had lunch with my husband. I feel very sorry for her. She pretends to be strong, but she's really very fragile. She pretends that she's confident, but she spends all her time wondering what other people think of her and her work. She must be a very lonely person. As you know, my dear, we women have a very keen sixth sense when it comes to detecting anyone who is a threat to our relationship. Don't you agree?"

Of course, I say, showing no emotion whatsoever. The aide looks impatient. The winner of the election is waiting for me.

"But she doesn't have a hope in hell," Marianne concludes.

Then she holds out her hand, which I dutifully shake, and she moves off without another word.

I SPEND the whole of Monday morning trying to call Jacob's private mobile number. I never get through. I block his number, on the assumption that he has done the same with mine. I try ringing again, but still no luck.

I ring his aides. I'm told that he's very busy after the elections, but I need to speak to him. I continue trying.

I adopt a strategy I often have to resort to: I use the phone of someone whose number will not be on his list of contacts.

The telephone rings twice and Jacob answers.

It's me. I need to see you urgently.

Jacob replies politely and says that today is impossible, but he'll call me back. He asks:

"Is this your new number?"

No, I borrowed it from someone because you weren't answering my calls.

He laughs. I imagine he's surrounded by people. He's very good at pretending that he's talking about something perfectly legitimate.

Someone took a photo of us in the park and is trying to blackmail me, I lie. I'll say that it was all your fault, that you grabbed me. The people who elected you and thought that the last extramarital affair was a one-off will be disappointed. You may have been elected to the Council of States, but you could miss out on becoming a minister, I say.

"Are you feeling all right?"

Yes, I say, and hang up, but only after asking him to send me a text confirming where and when we should meet tomorrow.

I feel fine.

Why wouldn't I? I finally have something to fill my boring life. And my sleepless nights will no longer be full of crazy thoughts: now I know what I want. I have an enemy to destroy and a goal to achieve.

A man.

It isn't love (or is it?), but that doesn't matter. My love belongs to me and I'm free to offer it to whomever I choose, even if it's unrequited. Of course, it would be great if it were requited, but if not, who cares. I'm not going to give up digging this hole, because I know that there's water down below. Fresh water.

I'm pleased by that last thought: I'm free to love anyone in the world. I can decide who without asking anyone's permission. How many men have fallen in love with me in the past and not been loved in return? And yet they still sent me presents, courted me, accepted being humiliated in front of their friends. And they never became angry.

When they see me again, there is still a glimmer of failed conquest in their eyes. They will keep trying for the rest of their lives.

If they can act like that, why shouldn't I do the same? It's thrilling to fight for a love that's entirely unrequited.

It might not be much fun. It might leave profound and lasting scars. But it's interesting—especially for a person who, for years now, has been afraid of taking risks and who has begun to be terrified by the possibility that things might change without her being able to control them.

I'm not going to repress my feelings any longer. This challenge is my salvation.

Six months ago, we bought a new washing machine and had to change the plumbing in the laundry room. We had to change the flooring, too, and paint the walls. In the end, it looked far prettier than the kitchen.

To avoid an unfortunate contrast, we had to replace the kitchen. Then we noticed that the living room looked old and faded. So we redecorated the living room, which then looked more inviting than the study we hadn't touched for ten years. So then we went to work on the study. Gradually, the refurbishment spread to the whole house.

I hope the same doesn't happen to my life. I hope that the small things won't lead to great transformations.

I SPEND quite a long time finding out more about Marianne, or Mme König, as she calls herself. She was born into a wealthy family, co-owners of one of the world's largest pharmaceutical companies. In photos on the Internet she always looks very elegant, whether she's at a social or sporting event. She's never over- or underdressed for the occasion. She would never, like me, wear jogging pants to Nyon or a Versace dress to a nightclub full of youngsters.

It's possible that she is the most enviable woman in Geneva and its environs. Not only is she heiress to a fortune and married to a promising politician, she also has her own career as an assistant professor of philosophy. She has written two theses, one of them—"Vulnerability and Psychosis Among the Retired" (published by Editions Université de Genève)—for her doctorate. And she's had two essays published in the respected journal *Les Rencontres,* in whose pages Adorno and Piaget, among others, have also appeared. She has her own entry in the French Wikipedia, although it's not often updated. There she is described as "an expert on aggression, conflict, and harassment in the nursing homes of French-speaking Switzerland."

She must have a profound understanding of the agonies and ecstasies of being human—so profound that she was not even shocked by her husband's "consensual sex."

She must be a brilliant strategist to have succeeded in persuading a mainstream newspaper to believe in her, an anonymous informer. (They are normally never taken seriously and are, besides, few and far between in Switzerland.) I doubt that she identified herself as a source.

She is a manipulator who was able to transform something that could have proved devastating to her husband's career into a lesson in marital tolerance and solidarity, as well as a struggle against corruption.

She is a visionary, intelligent enough to wait before having children. She still has time. Meanwhile, she can build the career she wants without being troubled by babies crying in the middle of the night or by neighbors saying that she should give up her work and pay more attention to the children (as mine do).

She has excellent instincts, and doesn't see me as a threat. Despite appearances, the only person I am a danger to is myself.

She is precisely the kind of woman I would like to destroy pitilessly.

Because she is not some poor wretch without a resident's permit who wakes at five in the morning in order to travel into the city, terrified that one day she'll be exposed as an illegal worker. Because she isn't a lady of leisure married to some high-ranking official in the United Nations, always seen at parties in order to show the world how rich and happy she is (even though everyone knows that her husband has a mistress ten years her junior). And because she isn't the mistress of a high-ranking official at the United Nations, where she works and, however hard she tries, will never be recognized for what she does because "she's having an affair with the boss."

She isn't a lonely, powerful female CEO who had to move to Geneva to be close to the World Trade Organization's headquarters, where everyone takes sexual harassment in the workplace so seriously that no one dares to even look at anyone else. And at night, she doesn't lie staring at the wall of the vast mansion she has rented, occasionally hiring a male escort to distract her and help her forget that she'll spend the rest of her life without a husband, children, or lovers.

No, Marianne doesn't fit any of those categories. She's the complete woman.

I'VE BEEN sleeping better. I should be meeting Jacob before the end of the week—at least that's what he promised, and I doubt he would have the courage to change his mind. He sounded nervous during our telephone conversation on Monday.

My husband thinks that the Saturday we spent in Nyon did me good. Little does he know that's where I discovered what was really troubling me: a lack of passion and adventure.

One of the symptoms I've noticed in myself is a kind of psychological nearsightedness. My world, which once seemed so broad and full of possibilities, began to shrink as my need for security grew. Why could that be? It must be a quality we inherited from when our ancestors lived in caves. Groups provide protection; loners die.

Even though we know that the group can't possibly control everything—for example, your hair falling out or a cell in your body that suddenly goes crazy and becomes a tumor—the false sense of security makes us forget this. The more clearly we can see the walls of our life, the better. Even if it's only a psychological boundary, even if, deep down, we know that death will still enter without asking, it's comforting to pretend that we have everything under control.

Lately, my mind has been as rough and tempestuous as the sea. When I look back now, it's as if I am making a transoceanic voyage on a rudimentary raft, in the middle of the stormy season. Will I survive? I ask, now that there is no going back.

Of course I will.

I've survived storms before. I've also made a list of things to focus on whenever I feel I'm in danger of falling back into the black hole:

- Play with my children. Read them stories that provide a lesson for them and for me, because stories are ageless.
- Look up at the sky.
- Drink lots of iced mineral water. That may seem simple, but it always invigorates me.
- Cook. Cooking is the most beautiful and most complete of the arts. It involves all our five senses, plus one more—the need to give of our best. That is my preferred therapy.
- Write down a list of complaints. This was a real discovery! Every time I feel angry about something, I write it down. At the end of the day, when I read the list, I realize that I've been angry about nothing.
- Smile, even if I feel like crying. That is the most difficult thing on the list, but you get used to it. Buddhists say that a fixed smile, however false, lights up the soul.
- Take two showers a day, instead of one. It dries the skin because of the hard water and chlorine, but it's worth it, because it washes the soul clean.

But this is working now only because I have a goal: to win the heart of a man. I'm a cornered tiger with nowhere to run; the only option that remains is to attack.

I FINALLY have a date: tomorrow at three o'clock in the restaurant of the Golf Club de Genève in Cologny. It could have been in a bistro in the city or in a bar on one of the roads that lead off from the city's main (or you might say only) commercial street, but he chose the restaurant at the golf club.

In the middle of the afternoon.

Because at that hour, the restaurant will be empty and we'll have more privacy. I need to come up with a good excuse for my boss, but that's not a problem. After all, the article I wrote about the elections was picked up by lots of other newspapers.

A discreet place, that's what he must have had in mind. But in my usual mania for believing whatever I want, I think of it as romantic. Autumn has already painted the trees many shades of gold; perhaps I'll invite Jacob to go for a walk. I think better when I'm moving, especially when I run, as proven in Nyon, but I doubt very much that we'll do any running.

Ha, ha, ha.

Tonight for dinner we had a cheese fondue that we Swiss call raclette, accompanied by thin slices of raw bison meat and traditional rösti potatoes with cream. My family asked if we were celebrating something special, and I said that we were: the fact that we were together and could enjoy a quiet dinner in one another's company. Then I took my second shower of the day and allowed the water to wash away my anxiety. Afterward, I slathered on plenty of moisturizer and went to the children's bedroom to read them a story. I found them glued to their tablets, which I think should be forbidden for anyone under fifteen.

I told them to turn their electronics off, and they reluctantly obeyed. I picked up a book of traditional stories, opened it at random, and began to read.

> During the ice age, many animals died of cold, so the porcupines decided to band together to provide one another with warmth and protection. But their spines or quills kept sticking into their surrounding companions, precisely those who provided the most warmth. And so they drifted apart again.
>
> And again many of them died of cold.
>
> They had to make a choice: either risk extinction or accept their fellow porcupines' spines.
>
> Very wisely, they decided to huddle together again. They learned to live with the minor wounds inflicted by their relatives, because the most important thing to their survival was that shared warmth.

The children want to know if they can see a real porcupine.

"Are there any at the zoo?"

I don't know.

"What's the ice age?"

A time when it was very, very cold.

"Like winter?"

Yes, but a winter that never ended.

"But why didn't they remove their prickly spines before they snuggled up together?"

Oh, dear, I should have chosen another story. I turn out the light and decide to sing them to sleep with a traditional song from a village in the Alps, stroking their hair as I do so. They soon fall asleep.

My husband brings me some Valium. I've always refused to take any medicine because I'm afraid of becoming dependent, but I need to be in top form tomorrow.

I take a ten-milligram pill and fall into a deep, dreamless sleep. I don't wake up all night.

I GET there early, and go straight to the clubhouse and out into the garden. I walk to the trees at the far end, determined to enjoy this lovely afternoon to the full.

Melancholy. That is always the first word that comes into my head when autumn arrives, because I know the summer is over. The days will grow shorter, and we don't live in the charmed world of those ice-age porcupines; we can't bear to be wounded by the sharp spines of others, even slightly.

We already hear about people in other countries dying of the cold, traffic jams on snowbound highways, airports closed. Fires are lit and blankets are brought out of cupboards. But that happens only in the world we humans create.

In nature, the landscape looks magnificent. The trees, which seemed so similar before, take on their own personalities and paint the forests in a thousand different shades. One part of the cycle of life is coming to an end. Everything will rest for a while and come back to life in the spring, in the form of flowers.

There is no better time than the autumn to begin forgetting the things that trouble us, allowing them to fall away like dried leaves. There is no better time to dance again, to make the most of every crumb of sunlight and warm body and soul with its rays before it falls asleep and becomes only a dim lightbulb in the skies.

I see him arrive. He looks for me in the restaurant and on the terrace, finally going over to the waiter at the bar, who points in my direction. Jacob has seen me now and waves. Slowly, I begin to walk back to the clubhouse. I want him to appreciate my dress, my shoes, my fashionable lightweight jacket, the way I walk. My heart may be pounding furiously, but I must keep cool.

I'm thinking about what words to use. What mysterious reason did I give for meeting again? Why hold back now when we know there's something between us? Are we afraid of stumbling and falling, like we have before?

As I walk, I feel as if I were entering a tunnel I've never traveled before, one that leads from cynicism to passion, from irony to surrender.

What is he thinking as he watches me? Do I need to explain that we shouldn't be frightened and that "if Evil exists, it's to be found in our fears"?

Melancholy. The word is transforming me into a romantic and rejuvenating me with each step I take.

I keep thinking about what I should say when I reach his side. No, best not to think and just let the words flow naturally. They are inside me. I may not recognize or accept them, but they are more powerful than my need to control everything.

Why don't I want to hear my own words before I say them to him?

Could it be fear? But what could be worse than living a sad, gray life, in which every day is the same? What could be worse than the fear that everything will disappear, including my own soul, and leave me completely alone in this world when I once had everything I needed to be happy?

I see the leaves falling, their shapes silhouetted against the sun. The same thing is happening inside me: with every step I take, another barrier falls, another defense is destroyed, another wall collapses, and my heart, hidden behind it all, is beginning to see and enjoy the autumn light.

What shall we talk about? About the music I heard in the

car on the way here? About the wind rustling the trees? About the human condition with all its contradictions, both dark and redemptive?

We will talk about melancholy, and he'll say that it's a sad word. I'll say, no, it's nostalgic, it describes something forgotten and fragile, as we all are when we pretend we can't see the path to which life has led us without asking our permission. When we deny our destiny because it's leading us toward happiness, and all we want is security.

A few more steps, a few more fallen barriers. More light floods into my heart. It doesn't even occur to me to try to control anything, only to experience this afternoon that will never be repeated. I don't need to convince him of anything. If he doesn't understand now, he will understand later. It's simply a matter of time.

Despite the cold, we'll sit out on the terrace so he can smoke. At first, he'll be on the defensive, wanting to know about that photo taken in the park.

We will talk about the possibility of life on other planets and the presence of God, so often forgotten in the lives we lead. We will talk about faith, miracles, and meetings that were planned even before we were born.

We will discuss the eternal struggle between science and religion. We will talk about love, and how it's always seen as both desirable and threatening. He will insist that my definition of melancholy is incorrect, but I will simply sip my tea in silence, watching the sun set behind the Jura Mountains and feeling happy to be alive.

Ah, yes, we will also talk about flowers, even if the only ones we can see are those decorating the bar inside, the ones that came from some vast greenhouse where they're produced en masse. But it's good to talk about flowers in the autumn. That gives us hope for the spring.

Only a few more feet. The walls have all fallen. I have just been reborn.

I reach his side, and we greet each other with the usual three kisses—right cheek, left cheek, right cheek, as demanded by Swiss tradition (although whenever I travel abroad, people are always surprised by that third kiss). I sense how nervous he is and suggest we stay out on the terrace; we'll have more privacy there and he can smoke. The waiter knows him. Jacob orders a Campari and tonic, and I order tea, as planned.

To put him at his ease, I start talking about nature, about trees, and about how lovely it is to realize that everything is constantly changing. Why are we always trying to repeat the same pattern? It's not possible. It's unnatural. Wouldn't it be better to see challenges as a source of knowledge, and not as our enemies?

He still seems nervous. He responds automatically, as if he wants to bring the conversation to a close, but I won't let him. This is a unique day in my life and should be respected. I continue talking about the various thoughts that occurred to me while I was walking, the words for which I had no control. I'm astonished to see them emerge now with such precision.

I talk about pets and ask if he understands why people like them so much. Jacob gives a conventional answer and then I move on to the next subject: Why is it so difficult to accept that people are different? Why are there so many laws trying to create new tribes instead of simply accepting that cultural differences can make our lives richer and more interesting? But he says that he's tired of talking about politics.

Then I tell him about the aquarium I saw at the school when I dropped my kids off that morning. Inside it was a fish, swimming round and round, and I said to myself: He can't remember where he began, and he will never reach the end. That's why we like fish in aquariums; they remind us of ourselves, well fed but incapable of moving beyond the glass walls.

He lights another cigarette. I see that there are already two cigarette butts in the ashtray. Then I realize that I've been talking for a very long time in a trance of light and peace without giving him a chance to express his feelings. What would he like to talk about?

"About that photo you mentioned," he says cautiously, because he's noticed that I'm in a particularly sensitive mood.

Ah, the photo. Of course it exists. It's engraved on my heart and will be erased only when God chooses. But come in and see with your own eyes, because the barriers protecting my heart fell away as I was walking toward you.

Now, don't tell me you don't know the way, because you've entered several times before, in the past and the present. Yes, I found it hard to accept at first, too, and I understand that you might be reluctant. We're the same, you and I. Don't worry, I'll lead you there.

After I have said all this, he delicately takes my hand, smiles, and then sticks in a knife:

"We're not teenagers anymore. You're a wonderful person and, as I understand, have a lovely family. Have you considered marriage counseling?"

For a moment, I feel disoriented. Then I get up and walk straight to my car. No tears. No good-byes. No looking back.

I FEEL nothing. I think nothing. I get straight into my car and drive, not knowing exactly where I should go. No one is waiting for me at the end of the journey. Melancholy has become apathy. I need to drag myself onward.

Five minutes later, I'm outside a castle. I know what happened here; someone breathed life into a monster that remains famous to this day, although few people know the name of the woman who created him.

The gate into the garden is closed, but so what? I can climb through the hedge. I sit on the cold bench and imagine what happened in 1817. I need to distract myself, to forget everything from before and concentrate on something different.

I imagine that year, when the castle's tenant, the English poet Lord Byron, decided to live here in exile. He was hated in his own country, and also in Geneva, where he was accused of holding orgies and getting drunk in public. He must have been dying of boredom. Or melancholy. Or rage.

It doesn't matter. What matters is that one day in 1817, two guests arrived from England: another poet, Percy Bysshe Shelley, and his nineteen-year-old wife, Mary. (A fourth guest joined them, but I can't remember his name right now.)

They doubtless talked about literature. They doubtless complained about the weather, the rain, the cold, the inhabitants of Geneva, their English compatriots, the lack of tea and whiskey. Perhaps they read poems to one another and praised one another's work.

They thought they were so special and so important that they decided to make a bet: they would return to that same place within a year, each with a book he had written describing the human condition.

Obviously, after the initial enthusiasm and conversation about how the human being is a complete aberration, they forgot about the bet.

Mary was present during that conversation. She wasn't invited to participate, first, because she was a woman, and, even worse, because she was very young. And yet that conversation must have marked her deeply. Why did she not just write something to pass the time? She had a subject, she simply needed to develop it and keep the book to herself when she had finished it.

However, when they returned to England, Shelley read the manuscript and encouraged her to publish it. Further, since he was already famous, he decided to submit it to a publisher and write the preface himself. Mary resisted, but in the end agreed, with one condition: her name should not appear on the cover.

The initial print run of five hundred copies quickly sold out. Mary thought it must be because of Shelley's preface, but, on the second edition, she agreed to allow her name to appear as author. Ever since, the book has remained a constant presence in bookshops around the world. It has inspired writers, theater directors, film directors, Halloween partiers, and those at masked balls. It was recently described by one well-known critic as "the most creative work of Romanticism and possibly of the last two hundred years."

No one can explain why. Most people have never read it, but almost everyone has heard of it.

It tells the story of Victor, a Swiss scientist, born in Geneva and brought up by his parents to understand the world through science. While still a child, he sees a lightning bolt strike a tree and wonders if that is the source of life. Could man create another human being?

And like a modern version of Prometheus, the mythological figure who stole fire from the gods in order to help mankind (the author used *The Modern Prometheus* as her subtitle, but few remember this), he begins to work to try and replicate God's greatest deed. Needless to say, despite all the care he takes, the experiment slides out of his control.

The title of the book: *Frankenstein*.

Dear God, of whom I think very little but in whom I trust in times of affliction, did I come here purely by chance? Or was it Your invisible and implacable hand that led me to this castle and reminded me of that story?

Mary met Shelley when she was fifteen. He was already married, but, undeterred by social conventions, she followed the man she considered the love of her life.

Fifteen! And she already knew exactly what she wanted. And knew how to get it, too. I'm in my thirties and wish for a different things every hour, but am incapable of fulfilling them . . . although I'm perfectly capable of walking through a romantic, melancholy autumn afternoon, thinking about what to say when the moment arrives.

I am not Mary Shelley. I'm Victor Frankenstein and his monster.

I tried to breathe life into something inanimate, and the result will be the same as in the book: spreading terror and destruction.

No more tears. No more despair. I feel as though my heart has given up beating. My body reacts accordingly, because I can't move. It's autumn, and the evening comes on quickly, the lovely sunset soon replaced by twilight. I'm still sitting here when night comes, looking at the castle and seeing its tenants scandalizing the bourgeoisie of Geneva at the beginning of the nineteenth century.

Where is the lightning bolt that brought the monster to life?

No bolt from out of the blue. The traffic, which isn't very heavy in this area, anyway, grows still thinner. My children will be waiting for their dinner, and my husband—who knows the state I'm in—will soon start to worry. But it's as if I have a ball and chain around my feet. I still can't move.

I'm a loser.

SHOULD someone beg forgiveness for harboring an impossible Love?

No, certainly not.

Because God's Love for us is also impossible. It's never requited at the time, and yet He continues to love us. He loved us so much that He sent His only son to explain how Love is the force that moves the sun and all the stars. In one of his letters to the Corinthians (which we were made to learn by heart at school), Paul says:

> Though I speak with the tongues of men and of angels, and have not charity, I am become as sounding brass, or a tinkling cymbal.

And we all know why. We often hear what seem to be great ideas to transform the world, but they are words spoken without feeling, empty of Love. However logical and intelligent they might be, they do not touch us.

Paul compares Love with Prophecy, with knowledge of the Mysteries, and with Faith and Charity.

Why is Love more important than Faith?

Because Faith is merely the road that leads us to the Greater Love.

Why is Love more important than Charity?

Because Charity is only one of the manifestations of Love. And the whole is always more important than the part. And Charity is also only one of the many roads that Love uses to bring man closer to his fellow man.

And we all know that there is a lot of Charity out there without Love. Every week, a "charity ball" is held. People pay a fortune to buy a table, take part, and have fun in their jewels and their expensive clothes. We leave thinking that the world is a better place because of the amount of money collected for the homeless in Somalia, the refugees from Yemen, or the starving in Ethiopia. We stop feeling guilty about the cruel display of poverty, but we never ask ourselves where that money is going.

Those without the right contacts to go to a charity ball or those who can't afford such extravagance will pass by a beggar and give him a coin. Fine. What could be easier than tossing a coin at a beggar in the street? It's usually easier than not doing so.

What a sense of relief, and for just one coin! It's cheap and solves the beggar's problem.

However, if we really loved him, we would do a lot more for him.

Or we would do nothing. We wouldn't give him that coin and—who knows?—our sense of guilt at such poverty might awaken real Love in us.

Paul then goes on to compare Love with sacrifice and martyrdom.

I understand his words better today. Even if I were the most successful woman in the world, even if I were more admired and more desired than Marianne König, it would be worth nothing if I had no Love in my heart. *Nothing.*

Whenever I interview artists or politicians, social workers or doctors, students or civil servants, I always ask: "What is your objective, your goal?" Some say: to start a family. Others say: to get on in my career. But when I probe deeper and ask again, the automatic response is: to make the world a better place.

I feel like going to the Mont Blanc Bridge in Geneva with a manifesto printed in letters of gold and handing it to every passing person and car. On it will be written:

I ask all those who hope to one day work for the good of humanity: never forget that even if you deliver up your body to be burned, you gain nothing if you have not Love. Nothing!

There is nothing more important we can give than the Love reflected in our own lives. That is the one universal language that allows us to speak Chinese or the dialects of India. When I was young, I traveled a lot—it was part of every student's rite of passage. I visited countries both rich and poor. I did not usually speak the local language, but everywhere the silent eloquence of Love helped me make myself understood.

The message of Love is in the way I live my life, and not in my words or my deeds.

In the letter to the Corinthians, Paul tells us, in three short lines, that Love is made of many elements, like light. We learn at school that if we pick up a prism and allow a ray of light to pass through, that ray will divide into seven colors, those of the rainbow.

Paul shows us the rainbow of Love just as a prism reveals to us the rainbow of light.

And what are those elements? They are virtues we hear about every day and that we can practice in every moment.

> Patience: Love is patient . . .
> Kindness: . . . and kind.
> Generosity: Love does not envy . . .
> Humility: . . . or boast; it is not arrogant . . .
> Courtesy: . . . or rude.
> Unselfishness: It does not insist on its own way.
> Good temper: It is not irritable . . . or resentful.
> Guilelessness: *or resentful.*
> Sincerity: It does not rejoice at wrongdoing, but rejoices with the truth.

All these gifts concern us, our daily lives, and today and tomorrow, not with Eternity.

The problem is that people tend to relate these traits to the Love of God, but how does God's Love manifest itself? Through the Love of man.

To find Peace in the heavens, we must find love on Earth. Without it, we are worthless.

I love and no one can take that away from me. I love my husband, who always supports me. I think I also love another man, whom I met in my youth. And while I was walking toward him, one lovely autumn afternoon, I dropped all my defenses and cannot rebuild them. I'm vulnerable, but I don't regret that.

This morning, when I was drinking a cup of coffee, I looked at the gentle light outside and remembered that walk, asking myself for the last time: Am I trying to create a real problem to drive away my imaginary ones? Am I really in love or have I simply transformed all the last month's unpleasant feelings into a fantasy?

No. God would never be so unfair as to allow me to fall in love like that if there were not some possibility for that love being requited.

But sometimes Love demands that you fight for it. And that's just what I will do. In the pursuit of justice, I have to ward off evil without exasperation or impatience. When Marianne is long gone and he is with me, Jacob will thank me for the rest of our lives.

Or he will leave again, but I will be left with the feeling that I fought as hard as I could.

I'm a new woman. I am pursuing something that won't come to me of its own free will. He is married and believes any false move might compromise his career.

So what do I need to concentrate on? On undoing his marriage without him realizing it.

I AM going to meet my first drug dealer!

I live in a country that has decided to happily shut itself off from the world. When you decide to visit the villages around Geneva, one thing becomes immediately clear: there is nowhere to park, unless you can use an acquaintance's garage.

The message is: don't come here, outsiders, because the view of the lake below, the majestic Alps on the horizon, the wildflowers in the springtime, and the golden hue of the vineyards in autumn, all are the legacy of our ancestors who lived here completely undisturbed. And we want to keep it that way, outsiders, so don't come here. Even if you were born and raised in the next city over, we are not interested in what you have to say. If you want to park your car, look for a big city, full of spaces for just that.

We are so isolated from the world that we still believe in the threat of major nuclear war. All Swiss buildings are required to have fallout shelters. A deputy recently tried to annul this law, but Parliament stood against it: Yes, there may never be a nuclear war, but what about the threat of chemical weapons? We must protect our citizens. So the costly fallout shelters continue to be built, and are used as wine cellars and storage spaces while we wait for the Apocalypse.

There are some things, however, that despite all our efforts to remain an island of peace, we cannot keep from crossing our borders.

Drugs, for example.

National governments attempt to control the suppliers and close their eyes to the buyers. We may live in paradise, but aren't we all stressed by traffic, responsibilities, deadlines, and boredom? Drugs stimulate productivity (cocaine) and relieve tension (hashish). So, not wanting to give a bad example to the world, we both prohibit and tolerate them at the same time.

But whenever the problem begins to take on noticeable proportions, some celebrity or public figure gets arrested with narcotics by "coincidence." The case winds up in the media as an example to discourage young people and show the public that the government has everything under control. Woe to those who refuse to comply with the law!

This happens, at most, once a year. But I don't believe that it's only once a year that someone important decides to break with routine and go to the underpass at Mont Blanc Bridge to buy something from the dealers who appear like clockwork every day. If that were the case, the dealers would be long gone for lack of clientele.

I arrive at the underpass. Families come and go while the suspicious characters stay put, not bothering one another or reacting, except when a young couple chatting in a foreign language strolls by, or when an executive in a suit walks through the underpass and turns back around immediately to look directly in their eyes.

The first time I walk through and reach the other side, where I take a sip of mineral water and complain about the cold to a person I've never seen before. She doesn't reply, immersed in her own world. I return and the same men are there. We make eye contact, but for once, there are a lot of people passing by. It's lunchtime and people should be at the overpriced restaurants that dot the neighborhood, trying to make an important business deal or wine and dine the tourist who came to the city in search of work.

I wait a bit and walk by a third time. I make eye contact again, and one man asks me to follow him with a simple nod. Never in my life did I imagine I would be doing this, but this year has been so unusual that I no longer find my behavior strange.

I feign an air of nonchalance and go after him.

We walk two or three minutes to the Jardin Anglais. We pass tourists taking photos in front of the flower clock, one of the city's landmarks. We cross by the station of the small train that runs around the lake, as though we were in Disneyland. Finally, we arrive at the jetty and look at the water like we're a couple gazing at the Jet d'Eau, the gigantic fountain that reaches up to one hundred forty meters high and has long been the symbol of Geneva.

He waits for me to say something, but I worry that my voice will shake in spite of my self-confident pose. I sit quietly and force him to break the silence:

"Ganja, crystal, acid, or blow?"

Okay, I'm lost. I don't know what to answer, and the man can tell he's dealing with a novice. I've been tested and I didn't pass.

He laughs. I ask if he thinks I'm with the police.

"Of course not. The police would know immediately what I'm talking about."

I explain that it's my first time doing this.

"You can tell. A woman dressed like you would never bother coming down here. You could ask your nephew or a work colleague for leftovers from their personal stash. That's why I brought you to the edge of the lake. We could have done the deal as we walked, and then I wouldn't be wasting so much of my time. But I want to know exactly what you're looking for, and if you need advice."

He wasn't wasting his time; he must have been dying of boredom just standing around in that underpass. In the three times I walked past, there hadn't been a single interested customer.

"All right, I'll repeat in terms you might understand: hashish, amphetamines, LSD, or cocaine?"

I ask if he has crack or heroin. He says those drugs are banned. I want to tell him that the ones he mentioned are also banned, but I bite my tongue.

It's not for me, I explain. It's for an enemy.

"You mean revenge? You want to kill someone with an overdose? Please, lady, find somebody else."

He begins to walk away, but I stop him and plead for him to listen to me. I note that desperation has likely already doubled the price.

As far as I know, the person in question doesn't do drugs, I explain. But she has seriously harmed my romantic relationship. I just want to set a trap for her.

"That's going against the ethics of God."

Will you look at that? Someone who sells addictive and possibly deadly products is trying to put me on the right path!

I tell him my story. I've been married for ten years, I have two wonderful children. My husband and I have the same kind of smartphone, and two months ago I grabbed his by accident.

"You don't use a security code?"

Of course not. We trust each other. Or maybe his has one, but it was deactivated at that moment. What's important is I found around four hundred texts and several photos of an attractive blond woman who is well-off, by the looks of it. I did what I shouldn't have. I made a scene. I asked him who she was, and he didn't deny it—he said she was the woman he loved. He was glad that I had found out before he had to tell me.

"That happens very often."

The dealer has gone from pastor to marriage counselor! But I keep going—because I am getting excited about the story I'm telling as I invent it. I asked him to move out. He agreed, and the next day he left me with our two children to go live with the love of his life. But she didn't take very kindly to this plan, as she thought it much more fun to be in a relationship with a married man than to live with a husband she didn't choose.

"Women! It's impossible to understand you!"

I think so, too. I continue my story: She said she wasn't ready to live with him and broke it off. As I imagine often happens, he came home begging for forgiveness. I forgave him. I actually wanted him to return. I'm a romantic woman, and I wouldn't know how to live without the person I love.

But now, after only a few weeks, I've noticed he's changed again. He's no longer foolish enough to leave his phone lying around, so there's no way to find out if they're back together. But I suspect they are. And the woman—that blond, independent executive, irresistibly charming and powerful—is taking what's most important in my life: love. Does he know what love is?

"I understand what you want, but it's really dangerous."

How can he understand if I haven't finished explaining?

"You want to set a trap for this woman, but we don't have the kind of merchandise you're asking for. To carry out your plan, you would need at least thirty grams of cocaine."

He grabs his smartphone, pulls up something, and shows it to me. It's a page from CNN's Money site detailing the price of drugs. I'm surprised, but discover it's a recent report on the difficulties facing the major cartels.

"As you can see, you'll need to spend five thousand Swiss francs. Is it worth it? Wouldn't it be cheaper to go over to this woman's house and make a fuss? Besides, from what I understand, she might not be guilty of anything."

He had gone from pastor to marriage counselor. And now, from marriage counselor, he's turned into a financial adviser, trying to keep me from needlessly spending my money.

I say I accept the risk. I know I'm right. But why thirty grams and not ten?

"It's the minimum amount to frame a person as a drug dealer. The penalty is much heavier than the one for users. Are you sure you want to do this? Because you could be arrested on the way to your house, or to that woman's house, and you'd have no way of explaining why the drugs are in your possession."

Are all drug dealers like this, or did I just fall into the hands of someone special? I'd love to spend hours chatting with this man. He's so experienced and knowledgeable. But apparently, he's very busy. He asks me to return in half an hour with the money in cash. I go to an ATM, surprised at my own naïveté. Of course drug dealers don't carry large quantities. Otherwise they'd be considered drug dealers!

I return and he is waiting. I hand over the money discreetly and he points to a trash can.

"Please don't leave the goods somewhere where the woman can find it, because she might get confused and wind up ingesting it. That would be a disaster."

This man is one of a kind; he thinks of everything. If he were the CEO of a multinational, he'd be earning a fortune in shareholder bonuses.

I think about continuing the conversation, but he's already walked away. I look back at the trash can. What if there's nothing there? But no, these men have a reputation to uphold and wouldn't do something like that.

Looking around, I walk over and grab the manila envelope inside, putting it in my bag and immediately taking a taxi to the newspaper offices. I'm going to be late again.

I paid a fortune for something that weighs almost nothing.

But how do I know that man didn't trick me? I need to find out for myself.

I rent two or three movies whose main characters are addicts. My husband is surprised by my new interest.

"You're not thinking of doing that, are you?"

Of course not! It's just research for the newspaper. By the way, I'll be home late tomorrow. I've decided to write an article about Lord Byron's castle and I need to stop by there. You needn't worry.

"I'm not worried. I think things have improved a lot since we spent that day in Nyon. We need to travel more, maybe at New Year's Eve. Next time we'll leave the children with my mother. I've been talking with people who understand this kind of thing."

The "thing" must be what he considers my depression. Who exactly have you been talking to? Some friend who will spill the beans the first time he has a little too much to drink?

"No, not at all. A marriage counselor."

How awful! Marriage counseling was the last thing I heard that terrible afternoon at the golf club. Have the two of them been talking behind my back?

"Maybe I caused your problem. I don't give you the attention you deserve. I'm always talking about work, or things we need to do. We've lost the romance needed to maintain a happy family. Caring about the children isn't enough. We need more than that while we're still young. Who knows, maybe we can revisit Interlaken, the first trip we took together after we met? We can climb part of the Jungfrau and enjoy the scenery from above."

A marriage counselor! That's all I need.

The conversation with my husband reminds me of an old saying: there is none so blind as the one who does not want to see.

How could he think he'd forsaken me? Where did he get

such a crazy idea? It's not as if I'm welcoming him to bed with open arms and legs.

It has been a while since we had an intense sexual relationship. In a healthy relationship, this is even more important for a couple's stability than making plans for the future or talking about the children. Interlaken takes me back to a time when we strolled around the city in the late afternoon—because the rest of the time we were locked up in the hotel, making love and drinking cheap wine.

When we love someone, we're not satisfied with knowing only the person's soul—we also want to understand the person's body. Is it necessary? I don't know, but instinct encourages us. There is no set time for it to take place, no rules to follow. Nothing beats that moment of revelation when shyness loses ground to boldness, and quiet moans turn into squeals and swearing. Yes, swearing—I have an overwhelming need to hear forbidden and "dirty" things when I've got a man inside me.

In these moments, the same old questions arise: "Am I squeezing too hard?" "Should I go faster or slower?" These questions might seem out of place or bothersome, but they are part of this act of initiation, understanding, and mutual respect. It is very important to talk while building a perfect intimacy. The opposite would mean silent and dishonest frustration.

Then comes marriage. We try to maintain the same behaviors, and sometimes we succeed—in my case, it lasted until I got pregnant the first time, which happened quickly. Until suddenly we realize that things have changed.

Sex, from now on, is only at night and preferably just before bedtime. As if it were an obligation, both parties accept without questioning whether the other is in the mood. If sex is skipped, suspicions arise, so it's best to stick to the ritual.

If it wasn't good, don't say anything, because tomorrow

may be better. After all, we're married. We have our whole lives ahead of us.

There is nothing else to discover, and we try to get as much pleasure as possible from the same things. This is like eating chocolate every day, without changing brands or trying new flavors: it's not a sacrifice, but isn't there anything else?

Of course there is: little toys you can buy at sex shops, swinger clubs, inviting a third person to join, or taking adventurous chances at parties hosted by unconventional friends.

To me, this is all very risky. We don't know what the consequences will be—it's better to leave things alone.

And so the days go by. We discover by talking with friends that the so-called simultaneous orgasm—where a couple becomes aroused at the same time, caressing the same parts and moaning in unison—is a myth. How can I have pleasure if I have to be paying attention to what I'm doing? Touch my body, drive me wild, and then I'll do the same to you—that would be more natural.

But most of the time that's not how it is. The communion has to be "perfect," or, in other words, nonexistent.

And careful with the moaning, so as not to wake the children.

Ah, I'm glad that's over, I was so tired and don't know how I managed. You're the best! Good night.

Until the day when one of the two realizes they need a break from the routine. But instead of going to swinger clubs, or sex shops full of gadgets we can't even figure out how to work properly, or to the home of wild friends who keep discovering new things, we decide to . . . spend some time without the children.

Plan a romantic getaway. With no surprises. Where everything will be absolutely, utterly planned and organized.

And we think this a great idea.

I create a fake e-mail account. I have the drugs, duly tested (followed by my vow *never to do that again*, because it felt great).

I know how to enter the university without being seen and plant the evidence in Marianne's desk. All I have to do is determine which drawer she won't be opening anytime soon, which is the riskiest part of my plan. But that's what the drug dealer suggested, and I should listen to the voice of experience.

I can't ask a student for help. I'll have to do it on my own. But other than this, I've got nothing else to do but nurture my husband's "romantic dream" and bombard Jacob's phone with my messages of love and hope.

The conversation with the drug dealer gave me an idea, which I put into practice: every day I send text messages of love and encouragement. This can work in two ways. The first is that Jacob will realize he has my support and that I'm not the least bit upset about our meeting at the golf club. The second, should the first fail, is if Mme König one day goes to the trouble of rummaging through her husband's phone.

I go online, copy something that seems intelligent, and press "send."

Since the election, nothing important has happened in Geneva. Jacob is no longer quoted in the press, and I have no idea what is happening with him. Only one thing has mobilized public opinion lately: whether or not the city should cancel the New Year's Eve party.

According to some deputies, the expense is "exorbitant." I was in charge of finding out exactly what that meant. I went to city hall and uncovered the amount: 115,000 Swiss francs, or what two people—me, and the colleague who works beside me, for example—pay in taxes.

In other words, with the tax money from two citizens who earn a reasonable but not extraordinary salary, they could make thousands of people happy. But no. We must save our money, because no one knows what the future has in store. Meanwhile, the city's coffers fill. We might run out of salt to dump on the streets this winter to keep the snow from turning into ice and causing accidents, or the sidewalks are always in need of repair. Everywhere you look there is roadwork and construction that no one can explain.

Happiness can wait. What's important is "keeping up appearances," which really means "don't let anyone realize that we are extremely wealthy."

I have to wake up early tomorrow and get to work. The fact that Jacob has ignored my messages has brought me closer to my husband. Yet I still intend to exact some revenge.

True, I have almost no desire to go through with it now, but I hate to abandon my plans halfway. Living is making decisions and dealing with the consequences. I haven't done that in a long time, and perhaps that's one of the reasons I'm lying here in the middle of the night and staring at the ceiling again.

Sending messages to a man who rejects me is a waste of time and money. I no longer care about his happiness. Actually, I want him to be really unhappy, because I offered him the best part of me and he suggested I try marriage counseling.

And because of that, I must put that witch in jail, even if my soul lingers in purgatory for centuries.

I *must*? Where did that come from? I'm tired, so tired, and I can't sleep.

"Married Women More Likely to Suffer from Depression than Single Women," claimed an article published in today's newspaper.

I didn't read it. But this year is turning out to be very, very strange.

When I was a teenager, everything in my life went exactly as I planned. I was happy . . . but now something has happened.

It's like a virus has infected the computer. The destruction has begun, slow but relentless. Everything is slowing down. Some large programs now require a lot of memory to open. Certain files—photos, documents—have disappeared without a trace.

We looked for the reason but found nothing. We asked friends who know more about these things, but they are unable to detect the problem, either. The computer is becoming empty, sluggish, and it is no longer ours. The undetectable virus now owns it. Sure, we can always switch to a new machine, but what about the things stored there, the things that took so many years to put in order? Are they lost forever?

It's not fair.

I don't have the slightest control over what is happening. My absurd infatuation with a man who, by now, must think he's being harassed. My marriage to a man who seems close, but who never shows his weaknesses and vulnerabilities. The desire to destroy someone I met only once, on the pretext that it will do away with my inner ghosts.

A lot of people say time heals all wounds, but that isn't true.

Apparently, time heals only the good things that we wish to hold on to forever. Time tells us, "Don't be fooled, this is reality." That's why the things I read to lift my spirits don't stay with me for very long. There is a hole in my soul that drains me of all positive energy, leaving behind only emptiness. I know the hole well—I have lived with it for months—but I don't know how to escape its hold over me.

Jacob thinks I need marriage counseling. My boss considers me an excellent journalist. My children notice a change in my behavior, but ask nothing. My husband understood what I was feeling only after we went to a restaurant and I tried to open my soul to him.

I take the iPad from the nightstand. I multiply 365 by 70. The answer is 25,550. That's the average number of days a normal person lives. How many have I already wasted?

People around me always complain about everything. "I work eight hours a day, and if I get promoted, I'll be working twelve." "Ever since I got married, I don't have any time for myself." "I searched for God and now I have to go to church services, Mass, and religious ceremonies."

Everything we seek so enthusiastically before we reach adulthood—love, work, faith—turns into a burden too heavy to bear.

There is only one way to escape this: love. To love is to transform slavery into freedom.

But right now, I can't love. I just feel hate.

And as absurd as this might sound, it gives meaning to my days.

I ARRIVE at the building where Marianne teaches her philosophy classes—an annex that, to my surprise, is located on one of the University Hospital of Geneva's campuses. Then I begin to wonder: Could this prized course on her CV be nothing more than an extracurricular with absolutely no academic weight?

Having parked the car at a supermarket, I walked about half a mile to get to this jumble of low buildings that sit in a beautiful green field with a little lake in the middle. Arrows indicate directions. Over there are institutions that, seemingly disconnected, are complementary if you stop to think about it: the hospital ward for the elderly and a mental hospital. The latter is in a beautiful building from the early twentieth century where psychiatrists, nurses, psychologists, and psychotherapists from all over Europe graduate.

I walk by something that, strangely, looks like the beacons one finds at the end of an airport runway. I have to read the sign beside it to figure out what it is. It's a sculpture called *Passage 2000,* a "visual song" comprising ten bars from railway crossings, all equipped with red lights. I wonder if the person who made it was one of the patients, but I discover when I keep reading that the work is by a famous sculptor. Let's respect art, but don't give me this about artists being normal.

It's my lunch hour—my only free time during the day, and when the most interesting things in my life always seem to happen—like meetings with friends, politicians, sources, and drug dealers.

The classrooms should be empty. I can't go to the campus restaurant, where Marianne—or Mme König—is probably casually flipping her blond hair to the side while the boys who study there imagine how they could seduce such an interesting woman and the girls gaze at her as a model of elegance, intelligence, and good behavior.

I go to the reception desk and ask for directions to Mme König's classroom. I am told that it is lunchtime (something there is no way I couldn't already know). I say that I don't want to interrupt her during her break, so I will wait for her outside her classroom door.

I am dressed normally, like a person you look at and immediately forget. The only suspicious thing is that I am wearing sunglasses on a cloudy day. I let the receptionist catch a glimpse of the bandages I put under the lenses. She will certainly conclude that I have recently had plastic surgery.

I walk toward the room where Marianne teaches, surprised by my composure. I imagined that I would be afraid, that I would give up halfway, but no. I'm here and I feel quite at ease. If I ever have to write about myself, I will do it for the same reason as Mary Shelley and her Victor Frankenstein: I just wanted to get out of a rut, find a better reason for my boring, unchallenging life. Her result was a monster capable of implicating the innocent and saving the guilty.

Everyone has a dark side. Everyone wants a taste of absolute power. I read stories of torture and war and see that those who inflict suffering are driven by an unknown monster when they are able to exert power, but turn into docile fathers, servants of the homeland, and excellent husbands when they return home.

I remember when I was young a boyfriend asked me to take care of his poodle. I hated that dog. I had to share the attention of the man I loved with it. I wanted *all* his love.

One day I decided to take revenge on that irrational animal, an animal that in no way contributed to the growth of humanity, but whose helplessness aroused love and affection.

I began attacking him in a way that would leave no trace by prodding him with a pin stuck on the end of a broomstick. The dog whined and barked, but I didn't stop until I got tired.

When my boyfriend arrived, he hugged and kissed me like always. He thanked me for taking care of his poodle. We made love, and life continued as before. Dogs can't talk.

I think of this as I make my way to Marianne's office. How could I have ever been capable of that? Because everyone is. I've seen men madly in love with their wives lose their heads and beat them, only to beg and sob for forgiveness immediately after.

We are incomprehensible animals.

But why do this to Marianne, when all she did was snub me at a party? Why come up with a plan and take the risk of buying drugs and planting them in her desk?

Because she's attained what I cannot: Jacob's love and attention.

Is that a good enough answer? If it were, 99.9 percent of people would be conspiring to destroy one another right now.

Maybe it's because I am tired of complaining. Because these sleepless nights are driving me mad. Because I feel comfortable in my madness. Because I won't get caught. Because I want to stop obsessing about this. Because I am seriously ill. Because I am not the only one. *Frankenstein* has never gone out of print, because everyone sees a bit of themselves in both the scientist and the monster.

I stop. *I'm seriously ill.* It's a real possibility. Maybe I should get out of here right now and find a doctor. I need to finish the task I've set out to do, but I will, even if the doctor then tells the police—he'll protect me with patient confidentiality, but at the same time expose an injustice.

I arrive at the classroom door, reflecting on the "whys" I've listed along the way. I go in anyway, without hesitation.

I find a cheap desk with no drawers. Just a wooden tabletop on turned legs. Something for laying down a few books, a bag, and nothing more.

I should have guessed. I'm frustrated and relieved at the same time.

The halls, previously silent, begin to show signs of life; people are returning to class. I leave without looking back, walking in the direction from where they came. There is a door at the end of the hall. I open it and exit at the top of a small hill across from the hospital for the elderly with its massive walls and—I'm sure—the heating running smoothly. I walk over and, at the reception desk, I ask for someone who doesn't exist. I am told the person must be somewhere else—Geneva must have more nursing homes per square meter than any other city. The nurse offers to look around for me. I say there's no need, but she insists:

"It's no trouble."

To avoid further suspicion, I agree to let her search. While she sits busily at her computer, I pick a book off the counter and leaf through it.

"They're children's stories," says the nurse, without taking her eyes off the screen. "The patients love them."

It makes sense. I open to a page at random:

> A mouse was always depressed because he was afraid of cats. A great wizard took pity on him and turned him into a cat. Then he started to be afraid of dogs, and so the wizard turned him into a dog. Then he began to fear tigers. The wizard, who was very patient, used his powers to turn him into a tiger. Then he was afraid of hunters. Finally, the wizard gave up and turned him back into a mouse, saying:

> "Nothing I do will help you, because you never understood your growth. You are better being what you always were."

The nurse is unable to find the imaginary patient. She apologizes. I thank her and prepare to leave, but apparently she is happy to have someone to talk to.

"Do you think plastic surgery helps?"

Plastic surgery? Ah, right. I remember the small pieces of adhesive tape under my sunglasses.

"Most patients here have had plastic surgery. If I were you, I would stay away. It creates an imbalance between the mind and body." I didn't ask her opinion, but she seems overcome with humanitarian duty and continues: "The aging process is more traumatic for those who think they can control the passage of time."

I ask her nationality: Hungarian. Of course. Swiss people never give their opinion without being asked.

I thank her for her trouble and leave, taking off the sunglasses and bandages. The disguise worked, but the plan did not. The campus is empty again. Now everyone is busy learning how to care, how to think, and how to make others think.

I take the long way back to my car. From a distance, I can see the psychiatric hospital. Should I be in there?

ARE WE all like this? I ask my husband after the kids have fallen asleep and we are getting ready for bed.

"Like what?"

Like me, who either feels great or feels awful.

"I think so. We're always practicing self-control, trying to keep the monster from coming out of his hiding place."

It's true.

"We aren't who we want to be. We are what society demands. We are what our parents choose. We don't want to disappoint anyone; we have a great need to be loved. So we smother the best in us. Gradually, the light of our dreams turns into the monster of our nightmares. They become things not done, possibilities not lived."

As I understand it, psychiatry used to call it "manic-depressive psychosis," but now they call it "bipolar disorder" to be more politically correct. Where did they get that name? Is there something different between the north and south poles? It must be a minority . . .

"Of course people who express those dualities are a minority. But I bet almost every person has that monster inside of them."

On one side, I'm a villain who goes to a campus to incriminate an innocent person without understanding the motive behind my hatred. On the other, I'm a mother who takes loving care of her family, working hard so that my loved ones want for nothing, but still without understanding where I get the strength to keep these feelings strong.

"Do you remember Jekyll and Hyde?"

Apparently, *Frankenstein* isn't the only book that has stayed in print since it was first published: *The Strange Case of Dr. Jekyll and Mr. Hyde*, which Robert Louis Stevenson wrote in three days, follows suit. The story is set in London in the nineteenth century. Physician and researcher Henry Jekyll believes that good and evil coexist in all people. He is determined to prove his theory, which was ridiculed by almost everyone he knows, including the father of his fiancée, Beatrix. After working tirelessly in his laboratory, he manages to develop a formula. Not wanting to endanger anyone's life, he uses himself as a guinea pig.

As a result, his demonic side—whom he calls Mr. Hyde—is revealed. Jekyll believes he can control Hyde's comings and goings, but soon realizes that he is sorely mistaken; when we release our dark side, it will completely overshadow the best in us.

The same is true for all individuals. That is how dictators are born. In the beginning they generally have excellent intentions, but little by little, in order to do what they think is for the "good" of their people, they make use of the very worst in human nature: terror.

I'm confused and scared. Can this happen to anyone?

"No. Only a minority lack a clear notion of right or wrong."

I don't know if this minority is all that small; something similar happened to me in school. I had a teacher who was the best person in the world, but suddenly he changed and left me completely bewildered. All the students lived in fear, because it was impossible to predict how he would be from day to day. But no one dared complain. Teachers are always right, after all. Besides, everyone thought he had some problem at home, and that it would soon be resolved. Until one day, this Mr. Hyde lost control and attacked one of my classmates. The case went to the school board and he was removed.

Since that time, I've become afraid of people who seem excessively sensitive.

"Like the *tricoteuses*."

Yes, like those hardworking women who wanted justice and bread for the poor, and who fought to free France from the excesses committed by Louis XVI. When the reign of terror began, they would go down to the guillotine square bright and early, guarding their front-row seats and knitting as they waited on those who had been condemned to die. Possible mothers, who spent the rest of their day looking after their children and husbands.

Knitting to pass the time between one severed head and the next.

"You're stronger than me. I always envied that. Maybe that's the reason I've never shown my feelings—so I won't seem weak."

He doesn't know what he's saying. But the conversation has already ended. He rolls over and goes to sleep.

And I'm left alone with my "strength," staring at the ceiling.

ONE week later, I do what I promised myself I would never do: see a psychiatrist.

I make three appointments with different doctors. Their schedules are packed—a sign there are more unbalanced people in Geneva than imagined. I say it's urgent, but the secretaries contend that everything is urgent, thank me for my interest and apologize, but they can't cancel other patients' appointments.

I resort to the trump card that never fails: I say where I work. The magic word "journalist," followed by the name of a major newspaper, can open as many doors as it closes. In this case, I already knew the outcome would be favorable. The appointments are made.

I don't tell anyone—not my husband, not my boss. I visit the first one—a strange sort of man with a British accent, who is adamant that he does not accept national health insurance. I suspect he is working in Switzerland illegally.

I explain, with all the patience in the world, what is happening to me. I use the examples of Frankenstein and his monster, of Dr. Jekyll and Mr. Hyde. I beg him to help me control the monster that is rising up and threatening to escape my control. He asks me what that meant. I don't want to provide details that might put me in a compromising situation, such as my attempt to have a certain woman wrongfully arrested for drug trafficking.

I decide to tell a lie: I explain that I am having murderous thoughts, thinking about killing my husband in his sleep. He asks if one of us has a lover, and I say no. He understands completely and thinks it is normal. One year of treatment, three sessions per week, will reduce this drive by fifty percent.

I am shocked! And what if I kill my husband before then? He replies that what is happening is a "transference," a "fantasy," and that real murderers never seek help.

Before I leave, he charges me 250 Swiss francs and asks the secretary to make regular appointments for me starting the following week. I thank him, say I need to check my schedule, and shut the door, never to return.

The second appointment is with a woman. She takes insurance and is more open to hearing what I have to say. I repeat the same story about wanting to kill my husband.

"Well, sometimes I also think about killing mine," she tells me with a smile. "But we both know that if every woman went through with her secret wishes, nearly all children would be fatherless. This is a normal impulse."

Normal?

After a long conversation, during which she explains that I am being "bullied" in my marriage, that without a doubt "I have no room to grow," and that my sexuality "is causing hormonal disturbances widely addressed in medical literature," she takes her prescription pad and writes down the name of a known antidepressant. She adds that until the medication takes effect, I will still be facing one month of hell, but soon all of this will be nothing more than an unpleasant memory.

As long as I continued taking the pills, of course. For how long?

"It really varies. But I believe that in three years you'll be able to reduce the dosage."

The big problem with using insurance is that the bill is sent to the patient's home. I pay in cash, close the door, and swear never to return to that place, either.

Finally, I go to the third appointment, another man in an office that must have cost a fortune to decorate. Unlike the first two, he listens to me attentively and seems to agree with me. I do indeed run the risk of killing my husband. I am a potential killer. I am losing control of a monster that I can't put back into its cage.

Finally, with great care, he asks if I use drugs.

Just once, I reply.

He doesn't believe me. He changes the subject. We talk a bit about the conflicts we're all forced to deal with on a daily basis, and then he returns to the drugs.

"You need to trust me. No one uses drugs just once. We're protected by doctor-patient confidentiality. I'll lose my medical license if I mention anything about this. It's better if we speak openly, before making your next appointment. Not only do you have to accept me as your doctor, but I also have to accept you as my patient. That's the way it works."

No, I insist. I don't use drugs. I know the laws and I didn't come here to lie. I just want to resolve this problem quickly, before I do any harm to people I love or who are close to me.

His pensive face is bearded and handsome. He nods before replying:

"You've spent years accumulating these tensions and now you want to get rid of them overnight. That does not exist in psychiatry or psychoanalysis. We're not shamans who magically drive out evil spirits."

Of course, he is being ironic, but he has just given me an excellent idea. My days of seeking psychiatric help are over.

POST *Tenebras Lux. After darkness, light.*

I am standing in front of the old city wall, a monument one hundred meters wide with towering statues of four men who are flanked by two smaller statues. One stands out from the rest. His head is covered, he has a long beard, and he holds in his hands what, in his time, was more powerful than a machine gun: the Bible.

While I wait, I think: If that man in the middle had been born today, everyone—especially Catholics, in France and around the world—would call him a terrorist. His tactics for implementing what he believed to be the ultimate truth remind me of the perverted mind of Osama bin Laden. Both men had the same goal: to install a theocratic state in which all who disobeyed what was understood to be the law of God should be punished.

And neither of the two hesitated to use terror to achieve their goals.

His name is John Calvin, and Geneva was his field of operations. Hundreds of people were sentenced to death and executed not far from here. Not only Catholics who dared to keep their faith, but also scientists who, in search of truth and the cures for diseases, challenged the literal interpretation of the Bible. The most famous case was that of Michael Servetus, who discovered pulmonary blood circulation and died at the stake because of it.

> Whoever maintains that wrong is done to heretics and blasphemers in punishing them makes himself an accomplice in their crime and as guilty as they. There is no ques-

> tion here of man's authority; it is God who speaks [. . .]. Wherefore does he demand of us a so extreme severity, if not to show us that due honor is not paid him, so long as we set not his service above every human consideration, so that we spare not kin, nor blood of any, and forget all humanity when the matter is to combat for His glory.

The death and destruction were not limited to Geneva; Calvin's apostles, likely represented by the monument's smaller statues, spread his word and his intolerance throughout Europe. In 1566 several churches in the Netherlands were destroyed and "rebels"—in other words, people of a different faith—were murdered. An enormous amount of artwork was thrown in the fire on the pretext of "idolatry." Part of the world's historical and cultural heritage was destroyed and lost forever.

And today my children study Calvin at school as if he were a great Illuminist, a man with new ideas who "freed" us from the yoke of Catholicism. A revolutionary who deserves to be revered by future generations.

After the darkness, light.

What went on in that man's head? I wonder. Did he lie awake at night knowing that families were being wiped out, that children were being separated from their parents, or that blood flooded the pavement? Or was he so convinced of his mission that there was no room for doubt?

Did he think everything he did could be justified in the name of love? Because that is what I doubt, and the crux of my current problems.

Dr. Jekyll and Mr. Hyde. People who knew him said that, in private, Calvin was a good man, capable of following the words of Jesus and making amazing gestures of humility. He was feared, but also loved—and could ignite crowds with that love.

As history is written by the victors, no one today remembers his atrocities. Now he is seen as the physician of souls, the great reformer, the one who saved us from Catholic heresy, with its angels, saints, virgins, gold, silver, indulgences, and corruption.

The man I'm waiting for arrives, interrupting my thoughts. He is a Cuban shaman. I explain that I convinced my editor to do a story on alternative ways of combating stress. The business world is full of people who behave with extreme generosity one moment and then take out their anger on those weaker. People are increasingly unpredictable.

Psychiatrists and psychoanalysts are booked solid and can no longer see every patient. And no one can wait months or years to treat depression.

The Cuban man listens to me without saying a word. I ask if we can continue our conversation in a café, since we're standing outside and the temperature has dropped significantly.

"It's the cloud," he says, accepting my invitation.

The famous cloud hangs in the city skies until February or March and is driven away only occasionally by the mistral, which clears the sky but makes the temperature drop even more.

"How did you find me?"

A security guard from the newspaper told me about you. The editor-in-chief wanted me to interview psychologists, psychiatrists, and psychotherapists, but that's been done a hundred times.

I need something original, and he might be just the right person.

"You can't publish my name. What I do isn't covered by national insurance."

I suppose that what he is really trying to say is: "What I do is illegal."

I talk for nearly twenty minutes, trying to put him at ease, but the Cuban man spends the whole time studying me. He has tanned skin and gray hair, and he's short and wears a suit and tie. I never imagined a shaman dressed like that.

I explain that everything he tells me will be kept secret. We're just interested in knowing if many people seek his services. From what I hear, he has healing powers.

"That's not true. I can't heal people. Only God can do that."

Okay, we agree. But every day we meet someone whose behavior suddenly changes from one moment to the next. And we wonder: What happened to this person I thought I knew? Why is he acting so aggressively? Is it stress at work?

And then the next day the person is normal again. You're relieved, but soon after the rug is pulled out from under you when you least expect it. And this time, instead of asking what's wrong with this person, you wonder what you did wrong.

The shaman says nothing. He still doesn't trust me.

Is it curable?

"There's a cure, but it belongs to God."

Yes, I know, but how does God cure it?

"It varies. Look into my eyes."

I obey and fall into some sort of trance, unable to control where I'm going.

"In the name of the forces that guide my work, by the power given to me, I ask the spirits who protect me to destroy your life and that of your family if you decide to turn me over to the police or report me to the immigration authorities."

He waves his hand a few times around my head. It feels like the most surreal thing in the world, and I want to get up and leave. But when I come to, he's already back to normal—neither friendly nor aloof.

"You may ask. I trust you now."

I'm a little frightened. But it really isn't my intention to harm this man. I order another cup of tea and explain exactly what I want. The doctors I "interviewed" say that healing takes a long time. The security guard suggested that—I weigh my words carefully—God was able to use the shaman as a channel to end a serious depression problem.

"We are the ones who create the messes in our heads. It does not come from outside. All you have to do is ask the aid of the guardian spirit who enters your soul and helps tidy the house. But no one believes in guardian spirits anymore. They are there watching us, trying to help, but no one calls on them. My job is to bring them closer to those in need and wait for them to do their work. That's all."

Let's say, hypothetically, that during one of these moments of aggression, a person devises a Machiavellian plan to destroy another person. Like slandering someone at work, for example.

"It happens every day."

I know, but when this aggression passes, when the person returns to normal, won't they be consumed by guilt?

"Sure. And over the years, this merely worsens their condition."

So Calvin's motto—after the darkness, light—is wrong.

"What?"

Nothing. I was rambling on about the monument in the park.

"Yes, there is light at the end of the tunnel, if that's what you mean. But sometimes, when the person crosses through the darkness and reaches the other side, he leaves an enormous path of destruction behind him."

Perfect, back to the subject of your method.

"It's not my method. It has been used for many years against stress, depression, irritability, suicide attempts, and the numerous other ways mankind has found to harm himself."

My God, I've found the right person. I need to keep my cool.

We could call it a . . .

". . . self-induced trance. Self-hypnosis. Meditation. Every culture has a name for it. But remember that the Medical Society of Switzerland doesn't look kindly upon these things."

I explain that I do yoga and that I still can't manage to reach the state where problems are sorted out and solved.

"Are we talking about you or a story for the newspaper?"

Both. I let down my guard because I know I have no secrets with this man. I was sure of it the moment he asked me to look into his eyes. I explain that his concern with anonymity is absolutely ridiculous—a lot of people know that he sees people at his house in Veyrier. And many people, including prison security guards, use his services. That's what the guy at the paper explained to me.

"Your problem is with the night," he says.

Yes, that's my problem. Why?

"At night, simply because it is night, we are able to revive our childhood terrors: the fear of being alone, the fear of the unknown. But if we can defeat these ghosts, we will easily defeat the ones that appear during the day. We will not fear the darkness because we are partners of the light."

I feel like I'm sitting with a schoolteacher who is explaining the obvious. Could I go to your house to do a . . .

". . . an exorcism?"

That hadn't occurred to me, but it is exactly what I need.

"There is no need. I see a lot of darkness in you, but also a lot of light. And in this case, I'm sure that in the end the light will overcome."

I'm on the verge of tears. The man is actually delving into my soul, and I can't explain exactly how.

"Let yourself get carried away by the night from time to time. Look up at the stars and try to get drunk on the sense of infinity. The night, with all its charms, is also a path to enlightenment. Just as a dark well has thirst-quenching water at its bottom, the night, whose mystery brings us closer to the mystery of God, has a flame capable of enkindling our soul hidden in its shadows."

We talk for almost two hours. He insists I need nothing more than to let myself be carried away—and that even my greatest fears are unfounded. I explain my desire for revenge. He listens without commenting or judging a single word. The longer we speak, the better I begin to feel.

He suggests we leave and walk through the park. At one of its gates are huge plastic chess pieces and several black and white squares painted on the ground. Some people are playing, despite the cold weather.

He hardly says anything more; I keep on talking nonstop, sometimes thankful and sometimes cursing the life I lead. We stop in front of one of the giant chessboards. He seems more attentive to the game than to my words. I stop whining and also start following the game, though it doesn't interest me one bit.

"Go all the way," he says.

Go all the way? Cheat on my husband, put the cocaine in my rival's purse, and call the police?

He laughs.

"Do you see these players? They always have to make the

next move. They can't stop in the middle, because that means accepting defeat. There comes a time when defeat is inevitable, but at least they fought until the end. We already have everything we need. There is nothing to improve. Thinking we are good or bad, fair or unfair, all that is nonsense. We know that today Geneva is covered by a cloud that might take months to go away, but sooner or later, it will leave. So go ahead and let yourself go."

Not one word to stop me from doing something I shouldn't?

"No. By doing what you shouldn't, you will realize it yourself. As I said in the restaurant, the light in your soul is greater than the darkness. But for this you must go all the way to the end of the game."

In my whole life, I don't think that I've ever heard such a preposterous piece of advice. I thank him for his time, ask if I owe him anything. He says no.

Back at the newspaper, the editor asks what took me so long. I explain that because it's a rather unorthodox topic, it took me a long time to get what I needed.

"And since it's not all that orthodox, might we be encouraging any unlawful activity?"

Are we encouraging unlawful activity when we bombard young people with incentives for excessive consumption? Are we encouraging accidents when we advertise that new cars can reach speeds of up to 250 kilometers per hour? Are we encouraging depression and suicidal tendencies when we publish articles on successful people without explaining how they got there and make everyone else convince themselves they're worthless?

The editor-in-chief doesn't want to discuss this. It could be interesting for the newspaper, whose headline piece of the day was "Chain of Happiness Raises 8 Million Francs for Asian Country." I write a six-hundred-word article—the most space they would give me—and it's all taken from Internet searches. I wasn't able to use anything from my conversation with the shaman that had turned into a treatment session.

JACOB! He's just risen from the dead and sends me a message inviting me for coffee—as if there weren't so many other interesting things to do in life. Where is the sophisticated wine taster? Where is the man who now holds power, the greatest aphrodisiac in the world?

But most of all, where is the teenage boyfriend I met back when anything was possible?

He married, changed, and sends a message inviting me for coffee. Couldn't he be more creative and suggest a nudist run in Chamonix? Maybe then I'd be more interested.

I have no intention of answering. I was given the cold shoulder and humiliated by his silence for weeks on end. Does he think I'll come running just because he gave me the honor of an invitation?

After I go to bed, I listen with headphones to one of the tapes I recorded of the Cuban shaman. When I was still pretending that I was just a journalist—and not a woman frightened by herself—I had asked if self-hypnosis (or his preferred term, "meditation") could make someone forget about another person. I broached the subject in a way that would allow him to understand "love" as "trauma by verbal attack," which was exactly what we were talking about at that moment.

"That is a somewhat murky area," he replied. "Yes, we can induce relative amnesia, but since this person is associated with other facts and events, it would be practically impossible to eliminate someone completely. What's more, forgetting is the wrong approach. You should face things head-on."

I listen to the whole tape, and then try to distract myself, making pledges and jotting down a few more things in my calendar, but nothing works. Before I go to sleep, I send a message to Jacob accepting his invitation.

I can't control myself, that's my problem.

I WON'T tell you I missed you because you won't believe me. I won't tell you I didn't reply to your messages because I'm afraid of falling in love again."

I really don't believe any of that. But I let him continue to try to explain the unexplainable. Here we are in a regular café, nothing special, in Collonges-sous-Salève, a village on our border with France that's located fifteen minutes from my work. The small handful of other patrons are truck drivers and workers from a nearby quarry.

I'm the only woman, except for the one working the bar, who walks from one end of it to the other, overly made-up and engaging the customers in witty banter.

"It's been a living hell since you showed up in my life. Ever since that day in my office when you came to interview me and we exchanged intimacies."

"Exchanged intimacies" is a figure of speech. I gave him oral sex. He did nothing to me.

"I can't say I'm unhappy, but I'm increasingly lonely, though no one knows. Even when I'm among friends, and the atmosphere and drinks are great, the conversation is lively and I'm smiling, all of a sudden, for no reason, I can't pay attention to the conversation. I say I have an important commitment and I leave. I know what I'm missing: you."

It's time to get my revenge: You don't think you might need some marriage counseling?

"I do. But I would have to go with Marianne, and I can't convince her. For her, philosophy explains everything. She's noticed I'm different, but attributes it to the elections."

The shaman was right when he said we must take things

all the way. At this moment, Jacob has just saved his wife from a serious drug-trafficking charge.

"I've taken on too many responsibilities and I'm not yet accustomed to it. According to her, I'll be used to everything soon. What about you?"

What about me? What exactly do you want to know?

All my efforts to resist fell apart the moment I saw him sitting alone at a table in the corner with a Campari and soda in front of him, and he smiled as soon as he saw me enter. We're like teenagers again, only this time we can drink alcohol without breaking any laws. I hold his icy hands—icy from cold or fear, I don't know.

I'm fine, I say. I suggest that next time we meet earlier—daylight savings time is over and it's getting dark fast.

He agrees and gives me a discreet kiss on the lips, anxious not to draw attention from the men around us.

"For me, one of the worst things are the beautiful sunny days this autumn. I open the curtains in my office and see people out there, some walking and holding hands without having to worry about the consequences. And I can't show my love."

Love? Did that Cuban shaman feel sorry for me and ask for some help from mysterious spirits?

I expected almost anything from this meeting, except a man opening his soul to me like he is doing now. My heart beats stronger and stronger—from joy, surprise. I won't ask why this is happening.

"See, it's not that I'm jealous of others. I just don't understand why they can be happy and I can't."

He pays the bill in euros, we cross the border on foot and walk toward our cars, which are parked on the other side of the street—i.e., Switzerland.

There is no more time for displays of affection. We say

good-bye with three kisses on the cheek and each one heads toward his or her destiny.

Just like what happened at the golf club, I am unable to drive when I reach my car. I put on a cowl scarf to protect me from the cold and start to walk aimlessly around the hamlet. I pass a post office and a hairdresser. I see an open bar, but would rather walk to unwind. I have no interest in understanding what is happening. I just want it to happen.

"I open the curtains in my office and see people out there, some walking and holding hands without having to worry about the consequences. And I can't show my love," he'd said.

And when I felt like no one, absolutely no one, was capable of understanding what was going on inside me—not a shaman, not a psychoanalyst, not even my husband—you materialized to explain it to me . . .

It's loneliness. Even though I'm surrounded by loved ones who care about me and want only the best, it's possible they try to help only because they feel the same thing—loneliness—and why, in a gesture of solidarity, you'll find the phrase "I am useful, even if alone" carved in stone.

Though the brain says all is well, the soul is lost, confused, doesn't know why life is being unfair to it. But we still wake up in the morning and take care of our children, our husband, our lover, our boss, our employees, our students, those dozens of people who make an ordinary day come to life.

And we often have a smile on our face and a word of encouragement, because no one can explain their loneliness to others, especially when we are always in good company. But this loneliness exists and eats away at the best parts of us because we must use all our energy to appear happy, even though we will never be able to deceive ourselves. But we insist, every morning, on showing only the rose that blooms, and keep the thorny stem that hurts us and makes us bleed hidden within.

Even knowing that everyone, at some point, has felt completely and utterly alone, it is humiliating to say, "I'm lonely, I need company. I need to kill this monster that everyone thinks is as imaginary as a fairy-tale dragon, but isn't." But it isn't. I wait for a pure and virtuous knight, in all his glory, to come defeat it and push it into the abyss for good, but that knight never comes.

Yet we cannot lose hope. We start doing things we don't usually do, daring to go beyond what is fair and necessary. The thorns inside us will grow larger and more overwhelming, yet we cannot give up halfway. Everyone is looking to see the final outcome, as though life were a huge game of chess. We pretend it doesn't matter whether we win or lose, the important thing is to compete. We root for our true feelings to stay opaque and hidden, but then . . .

. . . instead of looking for companionship, we isolate ourselves even more in order to lick our wounds in silence. Or we go out for dinner or lunch with people who have nothing to do with our lives and spend the whole time talking about things that are of no importance. We even manage to distract ourselves for a while with drink and celebration, but the dragon lives on until the people who are close to us see that something is wrong and begin to blame themselves for not making us happy. They ask what the problem is. We say that everything is fine, but it's not . . .

Everything is awful. Please, leave me alone, because I have no more tears to cry or heart left to suffer. All I have is insomnia, emptiness, and apathy, and, if you just ask yourselves, you're feeling the same thing. But they insist that this is just a rough patch or depression because they are afraid to use the real and damning word: loneliness.

Meanwhile, we continue to relentlessly pursue the only thing that would make us happy: the knight in shining armor who will slay the dragon, pick the rose, and clip the thorns. Many claim that life is unfair. Others are happy because they believe that this is exactly what we deserve: loneliness, unhappiness. Because we have everything and they don't.

But one day those who are blind begin to see. Those who are sad are comforted. Those who suffer are saved. The knight arrives to rescue us, and life is vindicated once again.

Still, you have to lie and cheat, because this time the circumstances are different. Who hasn't felt the urge to drop everything and go in search of their dream? A dream is always risky, for there is a price to pay. That price is death by stoning in some countries, and in others it could be social ostracism or indifference. But there is always a price to pay. You keep lying and people pretend they still believe, but secretly they are jealous, make comments behind your back, say you're the very worst, most threatening thing there is. You are not an adulterous man, tolerated and often even admired, but an adulterous woman, one who is sleeping with someone else and deceiving her husband, her poor husband, always so understanding and loving . . .

But only you know that this husband is unable to keep the loneliness at bay. Because something has been missing that even you don't know how to pinpoint, because you love him and don't want to lose him. But a shining knight promising adventure in distant lands is a much stronger lure than your desire for everything to remain as it is, even if at parties people stare at you and whisper among themselves that it would be better to tie a millstone around your neck and toss you overboard than let you be a terrible example.

And to make matters worse, your husband quietly puts up with everything. He doesn't complain or make a scene. He believes it will pass. You also know it will pass, but now it's stronger than you.

That's the way things go for a month, two months, a year . . . and everyone quietly puts up with it.

But it's not about asking permission. You look back and see that you also used to think like these people who have become your accusers. You also used to condemn those you knew were adulterers and imagined that if you lived somewhere else, the punishment would be stoning. Until the day it happens to you. Then you come up with a million excuses for your behavior and say you have the right to be happy, even for a little while, because dragon-slaying knights exist only in fairy tales. The real dragons never die, but you still have the right, just once in your life, to live out an adult fairy tale.

Then comes the moment you tried to avoid at all costs, one that you had been putting off for so long: the moment you must decide to stay together or to separate forever.

Along with this moment, however, comes the fear of making a mistake, no matter what decision you choose. And you hope someone will make the choice for you, throw you out of the house or bed, because it is impossible to go on like this. After all, we are no longer one person, we have become two or many, each completely different. And since you've never been through this before, you don't know where it will end. The fact is that now you are facing a situation that will make one person suffer, or two, or many.

But mostly it will destroy you, whatever your choice.

TRAFFIC is at a standstill. Today of all days!

Geneva, with fewer than two hundred thousand inhabitants, behaves as if it were the center of the world. And there are people who believe this and fly all the way from their own countries to host what they call "summits." These meetings usually take place on the outskirts of town, and traffic is rarely affected. At most, we catch sight of a few helicopters flying over the city.

I don't know what happened today, but they closed one of our main roads. I read today's papers, but not the city sections with the local news. I know that major world powers send their representatives here to discuss the threat of nuclear-weapons proliferation, "on neutral ground." And does this affect my life?

A lot. I can't afford to be late. I should have used public transportation instead of taking this stupid car.

Every year, Europe spends approximately 74 million Swiss francs (more than 80 million U.S. dollars) on hiring private detectives who specialize in following, photographing, and providing evidence that a client's spouse is cheating on them. While the rest of the continent is in crisis and companies are going bankrupt and laying off workers, the infidelity market has seen tremendous growth.

And it's not only the detectives who profit. Developers have created smartphone apps like SOS Alibi. The way it works is simple: at a set time it sends your partner a sweet message as though you were still at your office. So while you're between the sheets drinking glasses of champagne, a text pops up on the partner's phone letting them know you'll be late leaving work because of an unexpected meeting. Another app, Excuse Machine, offers a series of excuses in French, German, and Italian—and you can choose whichever is most convenient that day.

But besides detectives and programmers, hotels have really come out the winner. With the one in seven Swiss adults who are having an extramarital affair, according to official statistics, and considering the number of married people in the country, we're talking about four hundred fifty thousand individuals looking for a discreet room where they can meet. To attract customers, the manager of one luxury hotel once said, "We have a system that enables credit-card charges to appear as lunch in our restaurant." The establishment has become a favorite among those willing to cough up 600 Swiss francs for one afternoon. That is precisely where I'm headed.

After a stressful half an hour, I leave my car with the valet and run up to the room. Thanks to their e-mail service, I know exactly where to go without asking anything at the front desk.

From the café on the French border to where I am now, nothing more was needed—no explanations, no vows of love, not even another meeting—for us to be sure that this was what we really wanted. We were both afraid to think too much and back down, so the decision was made without questions or answers.

IT IS no longer autumn, it is spring. I am sixteen again, and he's fifteen. I've mysteriously regained my soul's virginity (since my body's is lost forever). We kiss. My God, I'd forgotten what this is like, I think. I've just been living in search of what I wanted—what and how to do it, when to stop—and accepting the same from my husband. It was all wrong. We were no longer completely surrendering to each other.

Maybe he'll stop now. We hardly ever went beyond kissing before. They were long and delicious, exchanged in a hidden corner of the school, although I wanted everyone to see and envy me.

He doesn't stop. His tongue tastes bitter, like a mixture of cigarettes and vodka. I'm embarrassed and tense; I need to smoke a cigarette and have a vodka for us to be on equal footing, I think. I push him away gently, go to the minibar, and down a small bottle of gin in one gulp. The alcohol burns my throat. I ask for a cigarette.

He gives me one, but not before reminding me it's a nonsmoking room. It feels so lovely to break the rules, even stupid ones like that! I take a drag and feel ill. I don't know if it's the gin or the smoking, but I go to the bathroom and toss the cigarette into the toilet, to be safe. He comes after me, grabs me from behind, and kisses the nape of my neck and my ears. His body is pressed against mine, and I feel his erection on my back.

Where are my morals? What will happen after I leave here and resume my normal life?

He pulls me back into the room. I turn around and kiss his mouth and tongue that taste like tobacco, saliva, and vodka. I bite his lips and he touches my breasts for the first time since high school. I take off my dress and throw it in the corner. For a split second, I feel a little ashamed of my body—I'm no longer the girl from that spring at school. We remain standing. The curtains are open and Lake Léman is the only barrier between us and the people in the buildings on the far shore.

I imagine someone sees us, and this arouses me even more than him kissing my breasts. I'm a slut, a whore hired by an executive to screw at a hotel, up for absolutely anything.

But this feeling doesn't last long. Once again I am sixteen, when I masturbated several times a day to the thought of him. I pull his head to my chest and ask him to bite my nipple, hard, and I cry out a little from pain and pleasure.

He is still dressed, and I am completely naked. I push his head and ask him to go down on me. Instead, he throws me on the bed, takes off his clothes, and gets on top. His hands search for something on the nightstand. This makes us lose our balance and we fall to the ground. A sure sign of a beginner—but we are beginners and we aren't ashamed of it.

He finds what he was looking for: a condom. He asks me to put it on with my mouth. I do, inexperienced and rather awkward. I don't understand the need for it. I can't believe that he thinks that I go around sleeping with everyone and might have something. But I respect his wish. I can still taste the unpleasant flavor of the lubricant covering the latex, but I'm determined to learn how to do it. I don't let it come across that it's the first time I've ever used one of those things.

When I finish, he flips me over and asks me to get on all fours. My God, it's happening! And I'm happy.

But he starts to take me in the behind instead of my vagina. It frightens me. I ask what he's doing, but he doesn't answer, just takes something else from the nightstand and puts it on my anus. I believe it's Vaseline, or something similar. Then he asks me to masturbate and, very slowly, he enters me.

I follow his instructions, again feeling like a teenager for whom sex is taboo. It hurts. Oh my God, it hurts a lot. I'm unable to masturbate—I just grab on to the sheets and bite my lips to keep from screaming in pain.

"Tell me it hurts. Say you've never done this. Scream," he orders.

Once again I obey him. It's almost the truth—I've done it four or five times and never liked it.

His movements increase with intensity. He moans with pleasure. Me, with pain. He grabs me by the hair like an animal, a mare, and his pace grows faster. He withdraws in a single motion, rips off the condom, turns me over, and comes on my face.

He tries to contain the moans, but they are stronger than his self-control. He slowly lowers himself on top of me. I'm frightened and also fascinated by it all. He goes to the bathroom, throws the condom in the trash, and returns.

Lying down beside me, he lights another cigarette and uses the vodka glass as an ashtray, resting it on my belly. We spend a long time staring at the ceiling, saying nothing. He caresses me. He is no longer the violent man from a few moments ago, but the young romantic who used to talk to me about galaxies and astrology in school.

"We can't leave any smell."

His words are a brutal return to reality. Apparently, it's not his first time. That explains the condom and the particulars that make sure everything stays as it was before we entered the room. I silently insult him and hate him, but I disguise it with a smile and ask if he has any tips for eliminating odors.

He says to take a shower when I get home before hugging

my husband. He also suggests that I throw away these panties, because the Vaseline will leave a mark.

"If he's home, run in and say you're dying to go to the bathroom."

I feel disgusted. I waited so long to act like a tigress and ended up being used like a mare. But that's life; reality never comes close to our teenage romantic fantasies.

Perfect, I'll do that.

"I'd like to see you again."

Right. All it took was this simple phrase to transform what seemed like hell, a mistake, a misstep, back into heaven. Yes, I would also like to see you again. I was nervous and shy, but next time will be better.

"Actually, it was great."

Yes, it was great. I just now realize that. We know this story is doomed to end, but it doesn't matter now.

I don't say anything more. I just enjoy this moment by his side and wait for him to finish his cigarette before getting dressed and going downstairs ahead of him.

I'll leave by the same door through which I entered.

I'll take the same car and I'll drive to the same place I return to every night. I'll run in, saying I have indigestion and need to go to the bathroom. I'll take a bath, removing what little of him remains on me.

And only then will I kiss my husband and my children.

WE DID not have the same intentions in that hotel room.

I was after a lost romance; he was driven by a hunter's instinct.

I was looking for the boy from my adolescence; he wanted the attractive and bold woman who had gone to interview him before the elections.

I believed my life could take another direction; he just thought that afternoon would mean something other than the boring and endless discussions at the Council of States.

For him it was just a simple, but dangerous, distraction. For me it was something unforgivable and cruel, a display of narcissism mixed with selfishness.

Men cheat because it's in their genetic code. A woman does it because she doesn't have enough dignity; in addition to handing over her body, she always ends up handing over a bit of her heart. A true crime. A theft. It's worse than robbing a bank, because if one day she is discovered (and she always is), she will cause irreparable damage to her family.

For men it is just a "stupid mistake." For women, it feels like a spiritual crime against all those who surround her with affection and support her as a mother and wife.

As I'm lying next to my husband, I imagine Jacob lying next to Marianne. He has other worries on his mind: political meetings tomorrow, tasks to complete, his busy schedule. While I, the idiot, am staring at the ceiling and remembering each second I spent in that hotel, watching the same porn movie over and over, in which I had the leading role.

I remember the moment I looked out the window and wished someone were watching us with binoculars—perhaps even masturbating while watching me be submissive, humiliated, taken from behind. Just the idea turned me on! It drove me crazy and led me to discover a side of myself of which I was altogether unaware.

I'm in my thirties. I'm not a child, and I thought there was nothing new about me left to discover. But there is. I am a mystery to myself; I opened the floodgates and I want to go further, try everything that I know exists—masochism, group sex, fetishes, everything.

I'm unable to say that I don't want any more, that I don't love him, or that it was just a fantasy created by my loneliness.

Maybe I don't actually love him. But I love what he has awakened inside me. He treated me with zero respect, left me stripped of my dignity. Undeterred, he did exactly what he wanted, while I strived, once again, to try to please someone.

My mind travels to a secret and unfamiliar place. This time I'm the dominatrix. He's naked, but now I'm the one giving orders. I tie up his hands and feet, and I sit on his face and force him to kiss my vagina until I can't take any more orgasms. Then I turn him over and penetrate him with my fingers: first one, then two, three. He moans with pain and pleasure while I masturbate him with my free hand, feeling the hot liquid run down my fingers. I bring them up to my mouth and lick, one at a time, before wiping them on his face. He begs for more. I say that's enough. I'm the one in charge!

Before I go to sleep, I masturbate and have two orgasms, one after the other.

IT'S THE same scene today as it is every morning: my husband reads the daily news on his iPad; the children sit ready for school; the sun streams through the window; and I pretend to be worried when I'm actually scared to death one of them suspects something.

"You seem happier today."

I seem happier, and I am, but I shouldn't be. My experience yesterday was a risk for everyone, especially for me. Is there some underlying suspicion in his comment? I doubt it. He believes everything I tell him. Not because he's a fool—far from it—but because he trusts me.

And that just makes me more upset. I'm not trustworthy.

Actually, yes, I am. I was led to that hotel on false pretenses. Is that a good excuse? No. It's awful, because no one forced me to go there. I can always claim that I was feeling lonely and wasn't getting the attention I needed, just understanding and tolerance. I can tell myself that I need to be defied, confronted, and questioned about what I do. I can claim that this happens to everyone, even if only in their dreams.

But deep down, what happened is very simple: I went to bed with a man because I was dying to do it. Nothing more. No intellectual or psychological justification. I wanted to screw. End of story.

I know people who married for security, status, and money. Love was the last thing on the list. But I married for love.

So why did I do what I did?

Because I feel lonely. Why?

"It's so nice to see you happy," he says.

I say that yes, I really am happy. The autumn morning is beautiful, the house is tidy, and I'm with the man I love.

He gets up and gives me a kiss. The children, even without quite understanding our conversation, smile.

"And I'm with the woman I love. But why are you telling me this now?"

Why not now?

"It's the morning. I want you to tell me that again tonight, when we're in bed together."

My God, who am I?! Why am I saying these things? So he won't suspect anything? Why don't I just behave like I do every morning and play the efficient wife tending to her family's well-being? What are these displays of affection? If I start to be too affectionate, it may raise suspicions.

"I can't live without you," he says, returning to his place at the table.

I'm lost. But, strangely, I don't feel the least bit guilty about what happened yesterday.

WHEN I get to work, the editor-in-chief commends me. The article I suggested was published this morning.

"We've received a lot of e-mails for the newsroom, praising the story with the mysterious Cuban man. People want to know who he is. If he allows us to print his address, he'll have work for quite a while."

The Cuban shaman! If he reads the newspaper he'll see he never told me any of what is in the article. I took everything from blogs on shamanism. Apparently, my crises aren't limited to marital problems; now I'm starting to slip professionally.

I explain to the editor-in-chief about the moment the shaman looked in my eyes and threatened me if I revealed who he was. He says I shouldn't believe in that sort of thing and asks if I can give his address to just one person: his wife.

"She's been pretty stressed."

Everyone's pretty stressed, including the shaman. I can't promise anything, but I'll talk to him.

He asks me to call *right now.* I do it, and I'm surprised by the Cuban man's reaction. He thanks me for being honest and for keeping his identity a secret and praises my knowledge on the subject. I thank him, tell him about the reaction to the article, and ask if we can arrange another meeting.

"But we talked for two hours! The material you have must be more than enough!"

That's not the way journalism works, I explain. What was published used very little from those two hours. Most of it I had to research. Now I need to approach the subject in a different way.

My boss is still standing next to me, listening to my side of the conversation and gesturing. Finally, when the shaman is almost ready to hang up, I insist that the article was lacking. I need to explore the female role in this "spiritual" quest, and my boss's wife would like to meet him. He laughs. I will never break the deal I made with him, but I insist that everyone knows where he lives and the days he works.

Please, take it or leave it. If you don't want to take the conversation further, I will find someone who will. There is no shortage of people claiming to be experts in treating patients on the verge of nervous breakdown. Your method is different, but you aren't the only spiritual healer in the city. Many others, mostly Africans, have contacted us this morning looking to bring visibility to their work, earn money, and meet important people who could protect them in the event of a possible deportation case.

The Cuban is reluctant at first, but his vanity and fear of competition finally speak louder. We arrange to meet at his house in the village of Veyrier. I'm eager to see how he lives—it will liven up the article.

We are in the small living room converted into an office in his home. On the wall are diagrams that look imported from India: the locations of energy centers, the soles of the feet with their meridians. Several crystals rest on top of a piece of furniture.

We've already had a very interesting conversation about the role of women in shamanist rituals. He explains to me that at birth we all have moments of revelation, and this is even more common with women. As any scholar can see, the goddesses of agriculture are always female, and medicinal herbs were introduced to cave-dwelling tribes by the hands of women. They are much more sensitive to the spiritual and emotional world, and this makes them prone to crises that doctors used to call "hysteria" and today are called "bipolar"—the tendency to go from absolute euphoria to profound sadness several times a day. For the Cuban man, the spirits are much more inclined to speak with women than with men, because they better understand a language that is not expressed in words.

I try to speak his language: Because of this oversensitivity, might there be the possibility of, say, an evil spirit driving women to do things we don't want?

He doesn't understand my question. I rephrase it. If women are unstable enough to go from happiness to sadness . . .

"Did I use the word 'unstable'? I didn't. Quite the contrary. Despite their heightened sensitivity, women are more steadfast than men."

Like in love, for example. He agrees. I tell him everything that happened to me, and I begin to sob. He is unmoved. But his heart is not made of stone.

"When it comes to adultery, meditation helps little or not at all. In this case, the person is happy with what is occurring. They are maintaining the security of their relationship at the same time they experience adventure. It's the ideal situation."

What leads people to commit adultery?

"That's not my area. I have a very personal view of the subject, but that shouldn't be published."

Please help me.

He lights some incense, asks me to sit in front of him with my legs crossed, and then settles into the same position. Previously severe, he now seems like a kind wise man, who is trying to help me.

"If married people, for whatever reason, decide to look for another partner, this does not necessarily mean that the couple's relationship is not doing well. Nor do I believe that sex is the primary motive. It has more to do with boredom, with a lack of passion for life, with a shortage of challenges. It's a combination of factors."

And why does this happen?

"Because, ever since we've moved away from God, we live a fragmented existence. We try to find oneness, but we don't know the way back; thus, we are in a state of constant dissatisfaction. Society prohibits and creates laws, but this does not solve the problem."

I feel lighter, as if I've already acquired a different outlook. I can see it in his eyes: he knows what he's saying because he's already been through it.

"I met a man who was impotent when he was with his lover. Yet he loved being by her side, and she also felt good next to him."

I can't control myself. I ask if this man is him.

"Yes. My wife left me because of it. Which is no reason for such a drastic decision."

And how did you react?

"I could have summoned spiritual assistance, but I would have paid for this in my next life. But I needed to understand why she had acted as she did. In order to resist the temptation to bring her back using magic, I started to study the subject."

Grudgingly, the Cuban man takes on a professorial air.

"Researchers from the University of Texas in Austin tried to answer the question so many people pose: Why do men cheat more than women when they know that this behavior is self-destructive and will cause the people they love to suffer? The conclusion was that men and women have exactly the same desire to cheat as their partner. It just happens that women have more self-control."

He looks at his watch. I ask that he please continue—perhaps he is glad to open up his soul.

"Brief encounters without any emotional involvement on the part of the man, and with the sole aim of satisfying sexual urges, enable the preservation and proliferation of the species. Intelligent women should not blame men for this. They try to resist, but they are biologically inclined to do it. Am I being too technical?"

No.

"Have you noticed how human beings are more frightened by spiders and snakes than by automobiles despite the fact that deaths from traffic accidents are much more frequent? This occurs because our minds are still living in caveman times, when snakes and spiders were lethal. The same thing happens with a man's need to have multiple women. In those times he went hunting, and nature taught him that preservation of the species is a priority; you must get as many women pregnant as possible."

And didn't the women also think about preserving the species?

"Of course they did. But while man's commitment to the species lasts, at most, eleven minutes, for the woman, each child means at least nine months of pregnancy. Not to mention having to take care of the offspring, feed it, and protect it from danger like spiders and snakes. So your instincts were developed differently. Affection and self-control became more important."

He is talking about himself. He is trying to justify what he did. I look around at those Indian maps, the crystals, the incense. Deep down we're all the same. We make the same mistakes and walk around with the same unanswered questions.

The Cuban man looks at his watch again and says our time

is up. Another client will be arriving, and he tries to keep his patients from crossing paths in the waiting room. He gets up and walks me to the door.

"I don't want to be rude, but please, don't look me up again. I already told you everything I had to say."

IT'S IN the Bible:

> It happened, late one afternoon, when David arose from his couch and was walking on the roof of the king's house, that he saw from the roof a woman bathing; and the woman was very beautiful. And David sent and inquired about the woman.
>
> And one said, "Is not this Bathsheba, the daughter of Eliam, the wife of Uriah the Hittite?" So David sent messengers and took her, and she came to him, and he lay with her. Then she returned to her house. And the woman conceived, and she sent and told David, "I am pregnant."

Then David ordered that Uriah, a warrior faithful to him, be sent to the battlefront on a dangerous mission. He was killed and Bathsheba went to live with the king in his palace.

David—the great example, the idol for generations, the fearless warrior—not only committed adultery, he also ordered the murder of his rival, betraying his loyalty and goodwill.

I don't need biblical justification for adultery or murder. But I remember this story from my school days—the same school where Jacob and I kissed in the spring.

Those kisses had to wait many years to be repeated, and when it finally happened, it was exactly as I *hadn't* imagined. It seemed sordid, selfish, sinister. But I loved it anyway and wanted it to happen again, as soon as possible.

Jacob and I meet four times in two weeks. The nervousness gradually disappears. We have both normal and unconventional intercourse. I'm still not able to live out my fantasy of tying him up and making him kiss me down below until I can't bear the pleasure, but I'll get there.

LITTLE by little, Marianne loses her importance. Yesterday, I was with her husband again, and that shows just how insignificant she is in all this. I no longer want Mme König to find out or even think of divorce, because this way I can have the pleasure of a lover without having to give up everything I've accomplished with hard work and self-control: my children, my husband, my job, and this house.

What will I do with the cocaine I've hidden, the cocaine that could be found at any moment? I spent a lot of money on it. I can't try to resell it; I would be one step away from the Vandoeuvres prison. I vowed to never use it again. I could give it as a gift to the people I know who like it, but my reputation could be affected, or, worse, they might ask if I can get them more.

Achieving my dream of getting Jacob in bed took me to great heights and then brought me back down to reality. I discovered that although I thought it was love, what I am feeling is merely a crush, destined to end at any moment. And I'm not the least bit concerned with maintaining it: I already got the adventure, the pleasure of the transgression, the new sexual experiences, the joy. All without feeling a drop of remorse. I am giving myself the present that I deserve after behaving for so many years.

I am at peace. At least I was until today.

After so many days of sleeping well, I feel like the dragon has again emerged from the abyss from where it had been exiled.

AM I the problem or is it the coming of Christmas? This is the time of year that depresses me the most—and I'm not referring to a hormonal disorder or the absence of certain chemicals in the body. I am glad that things aren't as over-the-top in Geneva as they are in other countries. I spent the holidays in New York once. Everywhere there were lights, tinsel, carolers, decorated windows, reindeer, bells, fake snowflakes, trees with ornaments in every size and color, smiles glued on everyone's faces . . . And me, absolutely sure that I was a freak and the only one to feel completely alien. Although I've never taken LSD, I imagine you would need a triple dose of it to see all those colors.

The most we see here is a hint of decoration on the main street, most likely for the tourists. (Buy! Take something from Switzerland to your children!) But I still haven't been by there yet, so this strange feeling can't be Christmas. There isn't a single Santa Claus hanging from a chimney, reminding us we should be happy the whole month of December.

I toss and turn in bed, as usual. My husband sleeps, as usual. Tonight we made love. This has become more frequent, I don't know if it's to cover up my affair or because my libido has been heightened. The fact is that I've been more sexually excited by him. He doesn't ask me questions when I get home late, and he doesn't show that he's jealous. Except for the first time, when I had to rush straight to the bathroom, I follow Jacob's instructions to eliminate all traces of odors and stained clothing. Now I always bring an extra pair of panties, take a shower at the hotel, and enter the elevator with flawless makeup. I don't show any nervousness or raise suspicions. Twice I ran into people I know, and I made sure to say hello and leave them asking: "Is she meeting someone?" It's good for the ego and absolutely safe. After all, if they're in the elevator of a hotel in the same city where they live, they're just as guilty as I am.

I fall asleep and then awake again a few minutes later. Victor Frankenstein created his monster, and Dr. Jekyll allowed his to come to the surface. This still doesn't frighten me, but perhaps I need to go ahead and lay down a few rules for my behavior.

I have a side that is honest, kind, caring, professional, and capable of keeping my cool at difficult moments, especially during interviews, when some subjects prove aggressive or evade my questions.

But I am discovering a more spontaneous, impatient, wild side, one that is not confined to the hotel room where I meet with Jacob and one that is beginning to affect my daily routine. I am more easily irritated when a salesperson chats with a customer even though there's a line. Now I go to the supermarket only out of necessity, and I've already stopped looking at prices and expiration dates. When someone says something I don't agree with, I make a point of responding. I discuss politics. I defend movies everyone hates and criticize those everyone loves. I love surprising people with ridiculous and out-of-place opinions. In short, I've stopped being the reserved woman I always was.

People have started to notice. "You're different!" they say. It's one step away from "You're hiding something," which soon turns into "You only need to hide if you're doing something you shouldn't."

I may just be paranoid, of course. But today I feel like two different people.

All David needed to do was order his men to bring him that woman. He didn't owe anyone an explanation. And when trouble arose, he sent her husband to the battlefront. It's different in my case. As discreet as the Swiss are, there are two situations when they become unrecognizable.

The first is in traffic. If someone lingers a fraction of a second to start his car after the light turns green, we immediately start to honk. If someone changes lanes, even with a turn signal flashing, he will always get a dirty look in the rearview mirror.

The second concerns the dangerous event of change, whether it's our house, job, or behavior. Here, everything is stable, everyone behaves as expected. Please don't try to be different or suddenly reinvent yourself, because you'll be threatening our whole society. This country worked hard to reach its "finished" state; we don't want to go back to being "under renovation."

MY ENTIRE family and I are at the place where William, Victor Frankenstein's brother, was murdered. For centuries, this was a swamp. After Calvin's ruthless hands turned Geneva into a respectable city, the sick were brought here, usually to die of hunger and exposure, and thus keeping the city from being infected by any epidemics.

Plainpalais is huge, the only spot in the city center with virtually no greenery. In winter, the wind is bone-chilling. In summer, the sun makes us drip with sweat. It's ridiculous. But since when have things needed a good reason to exist?

It's Saturday and there are antiques vendors with stalls scattered all around. This market has become a tourist attraction and even appears in travel guides as a "good thing to do." Sixteenth-century relics intermingle with VCRs. Antique bronze sculptures from the remote corners of Asia are displayed alongside horrible furniture from the eighties. The place is swarming with people. A few connoisseurs patiently examine a piece and talk at length with the vendors. The majority, tourists and onlookers, find things they will never need but end up buying because they're so cheap. They return home, use them once, and then put them in the garage, thinking: "It's completely useless, but it was a bargain."

I have to keep the children under control the entire time; they want to touch everything, from valuable crystal vases to fancy toys from the turn of the nineteenth century. But at least they're learning that intelligent life exists beyond video games.

One of them asks me if we can buy a metal clown with a movable mouth and limbs. My husband knows their interest in the toy will last only until we get home. He says it's "old" and that we can buy something new on the way back. At the same time, their attention is diverted by some boxes of marbles, which children used to play with in the backyard.

My eyes fixate on a small painting; it's of a nude woman, lying in bed, and an angel in the process of turning away. I ask the vendor how much it costs. Before telling me the price (a pittance), he explains that it's a reproduction done by a local unknown painter. My husband observes us without saying a word and, before I can thank the man for the information and move on, he's already paid for it.

Why did you do that?

"It represents an ancient myth. When we get back home I'll tell you the story."

I want to fall in love with him again. I never stopped loving him—I've always loved him and always will—but our life together is verging on monotony. Love can withstand this, but for lust, it's fatal.

I am going through an extremely tough time. I know my relationship with Jacob has no future and I've turned my back on the man with whom I've built a life.

Whoever says "love is enough" is lying. It isn't and it never has been. The big problem is that people believe what they see in books and movies—the couple that strolls along the beach holding hands, gazes at the sunset, and makes passionate love every day in nice hotels overlooking the Alps. My husband and I have done all that, but the magic lasts only one or two years, at most.

Then comes marriage. Choosing and decorating the house, planning the nursery for the children to come, kisses, dreams, a champagne toast in the empty living room that will soon be exactly as we imagined—everything in its place. Two years after the first child is born, the house has no more room and, if we add something, we risk looking like we live to impress others and will spend the rest of our lives buying and cleaning antiques (which will later be sold for a song by our heirs and eventually wind up at the Plainpalais market).

After three years of marriage, a person already knows exactly what the other wants and thinks. At dinner parties we are obliged to listen to the same stories we've heard time and time again, always feigning surprise and, occasionally, having to confirm them. Sex goes from being a passion to a duty, and that's why it becomes increasingly sporadic. Before long it happens only once a week—if that. Women hang out and brag of their husbands' insatiable fire, which is nothing but an outright lie. Everyone knows this, but no one wants to be left behind.

Then comes the time for the extramarital affairs. Women talk—do they ever!—about their lovers and their insatiable fire. There's an element of truth in this, because more often than not it's happening in the enchanted world of masturbation—just as real as that of the women who let themselves be wooed by the first man who appeared, regardless of his attributes. They buy expensive clothes and pretend to be modest, even though they're exhibiting more sensuality than a sixteen-year-old girl—the only difference being that the girl knows the power she holds.

Finally, the time comes to resign ourselves to the monotony. The husband spends hours away from home, wrapped up in work, and the wife dedicates more time than necessary to taking care of the children. We are at this stage, and I am willing to do anything to change it.

Love alone is not enough. I need to fall in love with my husband.

Love isn't just a feeling; it's an art. And like any art, it takes not only inspiration, but also a lot of work.

Why is the angel turning away and leaving the woman alone in the bed?

"It's not an angel. It's Eros, the Greek god of love. The girl in the bed with him is Psyche."

I open a bottle of wine and fill our glasses. He puts the painting above the unlit fireplace—often just a decorative feature in homes with central heating. Then he begins:

"Once upon a time there was a beautiful princess who was admired by all, but no one dared to ask for her hand in marriage. In despair, the king consulted the god Apollo. He told him that Psyche should be dressed in mourning and left alone on top of a mountain. Before daybreak, a serpent would come to meet and marry her. The king obeyed, and all night the princess waited for her husband to appear, deathly afraid and freezing cold. Finally, she slept. When she awoke, she found herself crowned a queen in a beautiful palace. Every night her husband came to her and they made love, but he had imposed one condition: Psyche could have all she desired, but she had to trust him completely and could never see his face."

How awful, I think, but I don't dare interrupt him.

"The young woman lived happily for a long time. She had comfort, affection, joy, and she was in love with the man who visited her every night. However, occasionally she was afraid that she was married to a hideous serpent. Early one morning, while her husband slept, she lit a lantern and saw Eros, a man of incredible beauty, lying by her side. The light woke him, and seeing that the woman he loved was unable to fulfill his one request, Eros vanished. Desperate to get her lover back, Psyche submitted to a series of tasks given to her by Aphrodite, Eros's mother. Needless to say, her mother-in-law was incredibly jealous of Psyche's beauty and she did everything she could to thwart the couple's reconciliation. In one of the tasks, Psyche opened a box that makes her fall into a deep sleep."

I grow anxious to find out how the story will end.

"Eros was also in love and regretted not having been more lenient toward his wife. He managed to enter the castle and wake her with the tip of his arrow. 'You nearly died because of your curiosity,' he told her. 'You sought security in knowledge and destroyed our relationship.' But in love, nothing is destroyed forever. Imbued with this conviction, they go to Zeus, the god of gods, and beg that their union never be undone. Zeus passionately pleaded the cause of the lovers with strong arguments and threats until he gained Aphrodite's support. From that day on, Psyche (our unconscious, but logical, side) and Eros (love) were together forever."

I pour another glass of wine. I rest my head on his shoulder.

"Those who cannot accept this, and who always try to find an explanation for magical and mysterious human relationships, will miss the best part of life."

Today I feel like Psyche on the cliff, cold and afraid. But if I can overcome this night and give in to the mystery and faith in life, I will awake in a palace. All I need is time.

THE BIG day finally arrives when both couples will be together at a reception given by an important local TV presenter. We talked about it yesterday in bed at the hotel while Jacob smoked his customary cigarette before getting dressed and leaving.

I couldn't turn down the invitation because I'd already sent my RSVP. So had he, and changing his mind now would be terrible for his career.

I arrive with my husband at the TV station, and we are told the party is on the top floor. My phone rings before we get in the elevator, and I am forced to leave the queue and stay in the lobby, talking with my boss, while others arrive, smiling at me and my husband and nodding discreetly. Apparently, I know almost everyone.

My boss says my articles with the Cuban shaman—the second of which was published yesterday despite having been written more than a month ago—are a big hit. I have to write one more to complete the series. I explain that the man doesn't want to speak with me anymore. He asks me to find someone else "in the industry," because there is nothing less interesting than conventional opinions (psychologists, sociologists, et cetera). I don't know anyone "in the industry," but as I need to hang up, I promise to think about it.

Jacob and Mme König walk by and greet us with a nod. My boss was just about to hang up, but I decide to continue the conversation. God forbid we have to go up in the same elevator! "How about we put a cattle herder and a Protestant minister together?" I suggest. "Wouldn't it be interesting to record their conversation about how they deal with stress or boredom?" The boss says it's a great idea, but it would be even better to find someone "in the industry." Right, I'll try. The doors have closed and the elevator is gone. I can hang up without fear.

I explain to my boss that I don't want to be the last one to arrive at the reception. I'm two minutes late. We live in Switzerland, where the clocks are always right.

Yes, I have behaved strangely over the last few months, but one thing hasn't changed: I hate going to parties. I can't understand why people enjoy them.

Yes, people enjoy them. Even when it comes to something professional like tonight's cocktail hour—that's right, a cocktail hour, not party—they get dressed up, put on makeup, and tell their friends, not without a certain air of ennui, that unfortunately they'll be busy Tuesday because of the reception celebrating ten years of *Pardonnez-moi* as presented by the handsome, intelligent, and photogenic Darius Rochebin. Everyone who's "anyone" will be there, and the rest will have to settle for the photos that will be published in the only celebrity magazine for the entire population of French-speaking Switzerland.

Going to parties like this gives status and visibility. Occasionally our newspaper covers this type of event, and the day after we'll receive phone calls from aides to important people, asking if the photos where they appear might be published and saying they would be extremely grateful. The next best thing to being invited is seeing your presence garner the spotlight it deserved. And there is nothing that better proves this than appearing in the newspaper wearing an outfit specially made for the occasion (although this is never admitted) and the same smile from all the other parties and receptions. Good thing I'm not the editor of the social column; in my current state as Victor Frankenstein's monster, I would have already been fired.

The elevator doors open. There are two or three photographers in the lobby. We proceed to the main hall, which has a 360-degree view of the city. It looks like the eternal cloud decided to cooperate with Darius and lifted its gray cloak; we can see the sea of lights below.

I don't want to stay long, I tell my husband. And I start chattering to ease the tension.

"We'll leave whenever you want," he interrupts.

The next moment we are busy greeting an infinite number of people who treat me as if I were a close friend. I reciprocate even though I don't know their names. If the conversation drags on, I have a foolproof trick: I introduce my husband and say nothing. He introduces himself and asks the other person's name. I listen to the answer and repeat, loud and clear: "Honey, don't you remember so-and-so?"

So cynical!

I finish greeting them, and we go to a corner where I complain: Why do people have a habit of asking whether we remember them? There's nothing more embarrassing. They all consider themselves important enough to be etched in my memory, even though I meet new people every day because of my job.

"Be more forgiving. People are having fun."

My husband doesn't know what he's talking about. People are just pretending to have fun. What they're really looking for is visibility, attention, and—every now and then—the opportunity to meet someone and close a business deal. The fate of people who think they're so beautiful and powerful as they walk down the red carpet lies in the hands of an underpaid guy from the news department. The paginator receives the photos via e-mail and decides who should or shouldn't appear in our small world of traditions and conventions. He is the one who places images of people of interest in the paper, leaving a small space for the famous photo with an overview of the party (or cocktail hour, or dinner, or reception). There, with a little luck, one or another might be recognized among the anonymous people who consider themselves very important.

Darius takes the stage and begins to share his experiences with all the important people he interviewed during his program's ten-year span. I'm able to relax a bit and go to one of the windows with my husband. My internal radar already detected Jacob and Mme König. I want distance, and I imagine Jacob does, too.

"Is there something wrong?"

I knew it. Are you Dr. Jekyll or Mr. Hyde today? Victor Frankenstein or his monster?

No, darling. I'm just avoiding the man I went to bed with yesterday. I suspect that everyone in this room knows it, and that the word "lovers" is written on our foreheads.

I smile and say something he's tired of hearing, that I'm too old to go to parties. I would love to be home right now, taking care of our children instead of having left them with a babysitter. I'm not much of a drinker—I already get confused with all these people saying hello to me and making conversation. I have to feign interest in what they're saying and respond with a question before I can finally put the hors d'oeuvre in my mouth and finish chewing without seeming rude.

A screen is lowered and a video clip starts, featuring the most important guests who've been on the program. I've worked with some of them, but most of them are foreigners visiting Geneva. As we all know, there's always someone important in this city, and going on the show is obligatory.

"Let's leave, then. He already saw you. We've done our social duty. Let's rent a movie and enjoy the rest of the night together."

No. We'll stay a little longer, because Jacob and Mme König

are here. It might seem suspicious to leave the party before the ceremony ends. Darius starts calling some of his show's guests to the stage, and they make a short statement about the experience. I nearly die of boredom. Unaccompanied men start looking around, discreetly seeking single women. The women, in turn, look at one another: how they're dressed, what makeup they're wearing, if they're here with husbands or lovers.

I look out at the city, lost in absent thoughts, just waiting for time to pass so we can leave quietly without arousing suspicion.

"It's you!"

Me?

"Darling, he's calling your name!"

Darius just invited me to the stage and I hadn't heard. Yes, I had been on his show with the ex-president of Switzerland to talk about human rights. But I'm not that important. I never imagined this; it hadn't been arranged, and I didn't prepare anything to say.

But Darius gestures to me. The people all look my way, smiling. I walk toward him. I've regained my composure and am secretly happy, because Marianne wasn't called, nor will she be. Jacob wasn't called up, either, because the idea is for the evening to be enjoyable, not filled with political speeches.

I climb the makeshift stage—it's a staircase linking the two areas of the hall at the top of the TV tower—give Darius a kiss, and start telling an uninteresting story about when I went on the show. The men continue their hunt, and the women continue looking at one another. Those nearest the stage pretend to be interested in what I'm saying. I keep my eyes on my husband; everyone who speaks in public has to choose someone to serve as support.

In the middle of my impromptu speech, I see something that absolutely should not happen: Jacob and Marianne König are standing next to my husband. All this had to have happened in the less than two minutes it took me to get to the stage and start the speech that, at this point, is already making the waiters circulate and most of the guests look away from the stage in search of something more attractive.

I say thank you as quickly as possible. The guests applaud. Darius gives me a kiss. I try to get to my husband and the Königs, but am waylaid by people who praise me for things I didn't say and claim I was wonderful. They're delighted with the series of articles on shamanism and suggest topics, hand me business cards, and discreetly offer themselves as "sources" on something that could be "very interesting." All this takes about ten minutes. When I finally approach my destination, the three are smiling. They congratulate me, say I'm a great public speaker, and deliver the bad news:

"I explained to them that you're tired and that our children are with the babysitter," my husband says, "but Mme König insists on having dinner together."

"I do. I suppose no one here has had dinner?" says Marianne.

Jacob has a fake smile on his face and agrees like a lamb to the slaughter.

In a split second, two hundred thousand excuses run through my head. But why? I have a fair amount of cocaine ready to be used at any moment, and what better than this "opportunity" to see if I'll carry out my plan.

Besides, I have a morbid curiosity to see how this dinner goes.

It would be our pleasure, Mme König.

Marianne chooses the restaurant at Hotel Les Armures, which shows a certain lack of originality, as that's where everyone usually takes their foreign visitors. The fondue is excellent, the staff strives to speak every language possible, and it's located in the heart of the old city . . . *but* for someone who lives in Geneva, it is definitely nothing new.

We arrive after the Königs. Jacob is outside, enduring the cold in the name of his nicotine addiction. Marianne has already gone in. I suggest my husband also go in and keep her company while I wait for Mr. König to finish smoking. He says that the reverse would be better, but I insist—it wouldn't be polite to leave two women alone at the table, even if just for a few minutes.

"The invitation caught me off guard, too," says Jacob, as soon as my husband is gone.

I try to act as though nothing is wrong. Are you feeling guilty? Worried about a potential end to your unhappy marriage (with that stone-cold bitch, I'd like to add)?

"It's not about that. It's that—"

We're interrupted by the bitch. A devilish grin on her lips, she greets me (again!) with the three customary pecks on the cheek and *orders* her husband to put out his cigarette and come inside. I read between the lines: I'm suspicious of you two and think you must be planning something, but look, I'm clever, much more intelligent than you think.

We order the usual: fondue and raclette. My husband says he's tired of eating cheese and picks something different: a sausage that is on the visitor menu. We also order wine, but Jacob doesn't sniff, swirl, taste, and nod—that was just a dumb way of impressing me on the first day. While we wait for the food and make small talk, we finish the first bottle, which is soon replaced by a second. I ask my husband not to drink anymore, or we'll have to leave the car again, and we're much farther away from home than we were the previous time.

The food arrives. We open a third bottle of wine. The small talk continues; Jacob's new routine as a member of the Council of States, congratulations for my two articles on stress ("a rather unusual approach"), and if it's true the price of real estate will fall now that banking secrecy is disappearing and if the thousands of bankers will go with it. They are moving to Singapore or Dubai, where we spend the holiday season.

I keep waiting for the bull to enter the arena. But it doesn't, and I lower my guard. I drink a bit more than I should and start to feel relaxed and cheerful. Then the doors swing wide open.

"The other day I was talking with some friends about the stupid feeling of jealousy," says Marianne König. "What do you think about it?"

What do we think about a topic that no one talks about at dinner? The bitch knows how to choose her words well. She must have spent the whole day thinking about it. She called jealousy a "stupid feeling," intending to leave me more exposed and vulnerable.

"I grew up witnessing terrible displays of jealousy at home," says my husband.

What? He's talking about his private life? To a stranger?

"So I promised myself I would never let that happen to me if I ever got married. It was hard at first, because our instinct is to control everything, even the uncontrollable, like love and fidelity. But I did it. And my wife, who meets with other people every day and sometimes comes home later than usual, has never heard a criticism or an insinuation from me."

I've never heard this explanation. I didn't know he'd grown up with jealousy all around him. The bitch manages to make everyone obey her command: let's have dinner, put out your cigarette, talk about the topic I picked.

There are two reasons for what my husband just said. The first is that he is suspicious of her invitation and is trying to protect me. The second: he is telling me, in front of everyone, how important I am to him. I reach out my hand and touch his. I never imagined this. I thought he simply wasn't interested in what I did.

"And what about you, Linda? Don't you get jealous of your husband?"

Me?

Of course not. I trust him completely. I think jealousy is for sick, insecure people with no self-esteem, people who feel inferior and believe anyone can threaten their relationship. And you?

Marianne is caught in her own trap.

"Like I said, I think it's a stupid feeling."

Yes, you already said that. But if you found out your husband was cheating, what would you do?

Jacob goes pale. He restrains himself from drinking the entire contents of his wineglass.

"I believe my husband meets insecure people every day who must be dying of boredom in their own marriage and are destined to have a mediocre and repetitive life. I imagine there are some people like that in your line of work, too, who will go from junior reporter straight to retirement . . ."

"Many," I reply with zero emotion in my voice. I help myself to more fondue. She stares me right in the eyes. *I know* you're talking about me, but I don't want my husband to suspect anything. I don't care one bit about her and Jacob, who must have confessed everything, unable to stand the pressure.

My cool surprises me. Maybe it's the wine or the monster having fun with all this. Maybe it's the immense pleasure of being able to confront a woman who thinks she knows everything. "Go on," I say, as I dunk the piece of bread in the melted cheese.

"As you all know, these unloved women aren't a threat to

me. Unlike you, I don't have complete trust in Jacob. I know he's already cheated on me a few times. The flesh is weak . . ."

Jacob laughs nervously and has another sip of wine. The bottle's empty; Marianne motions to the waiter to bring another.

". . . but I try to see it as part of a normal relationship. If my man wasn't desired and pursued by these sluts, then he must be completely uninteresting. Instead of jealousy, you know what I feel? Horniness. I often take off my clothes, approach him naked, spread my legs, and ask him to do to me exactly what he did with them. Sometimes I ask him to tell me how it was, and this makes me come many times."

"That's all in Marianne's fantasies," says Jacob, rather unconvincingly. "She makes these things up. The other day she asked if I would like to go to a swingers club in Lausanne."

He's not joking, of course, but everyone laughs, including her.

To my horror, I discover that Jacob is enjoying being labeled the "unfaithful male." My husband seems very interested in Marianne's reply and asks her to talk a bit more about the arousal she gets from knowing about the extramarital affairs. He asks for the address of the swingers club and gazes at me, his eyes shining. He says it's about time we tried something different. I don't know if he's trying to manage the almost unbearable atmosphere at the table or if he is actually interested in trying. Marianne says she doesn't know the address, but if he gives her his phone number, she'll send it to him by text.

Time to spring into action. I say that, in general, jealous people will try to show exactly the opposite in public. They love to make insinuations and see if they can get some information about their partner's behavior, but are naïve to think they'll succeed. I, for example, could be having an affair with your husband and you would never know, because I'm not stupid enough to fall for that trap.

My tone changes slightly. My husband looks at me, surprised at my answer.

"Darling, don't you think that's going a little far?"

No, I don't. I'm not the one who started this conversation, and I don't know what Mme König is driving at. But ever since we got here she hasn't stopped insinuating things, and I'm sick of it. By the way, have you noticed how she's been staring at me the whole time we've been talking about something that's of no interest to anyone at this table but her?

Marianne looks at me, stunned. I think she didn't expect a reaction because she's used to controlling everything.

I say that I've met a lot of people who are driven by obsessive jealousy, and not because they think their husband or wife is committing adultery, but because they would like to be the center of attention all the time, and they're not. Jacob calls the waiter and asks for the bill. Great. After all, they were the ones who invited us and who should bear the expense.

I look at my watch and pretend to be greatly surprised; it's already past the time we gave the babysitter! I get up, thank them for dinner, and go to the cloakroom to get my coat. The conversation has already shifted to children and the responsibilities they bring.

"Do you think she really thought I was talking about her?" I hear Marianne asking my husband.

"Of course not. There would be no reason for that."

We go out into the cold air, not saying much. I'm angry, anxious, and I volunteer without being prompted that yes, she was talking about me, and that that woman is so neurotic that on election day she also made several insinuations. She's always wanting to show off—she must be dying of jealousy over the jerk whose "proper behavior" she controls with an iron fist so he has some future in politics, even though she's really the one who'd like to be campaigning for what is right or wrong.

My husband says that I've had too much to drink and should calm down.

We walk in front of a cathedral. Mist covers the city again and makes everything look like we're in a horror movie. I imagine Marianne waiting for me in a corner with a dagger, like in the days Geneva was a medieval city and in constant battle with the French.

Neither the cold nor the walk calms me down. We get the car, and when we arrive home I go directly to the bedroom and swallow two Valiums while my husband pays the babysitter and puts the kids to bed.

I sleep for ten hours straight. The next day, when I get up for the usual morning routine, I start to think my husband is a little less affectionate. It's almost imperceptible, but still something yesterday made him uncomfortable. I'm not sure what to do—I've never taken two tranquilizers at once, and am experiencing a lethargy that's nothing like the one loneliness and unhappiness caused.

I leave for work and automatically check my phone. There's a text from Jacob. I'm hesitant to open it, but curiosity is greater than hate.

It was sent this morning, very early.

"You blew it. She had no idea that there was something between us, but now she's sure. You fell into a trap she didn't set."

I HAVE to stop by the damn supermarket to buy groceries, feeling frustrated and unloved. Marianne is right; I'm nothing more than a sexual hobby for the stupid dog sleeping in her bed. I drive dangerously because I can't stop crying, the tears keeping me from seeing the other cars clearly. I hear honking and complaints. I try to slow down; I hear more honking and more complaints.

If it was stupid to let Marianne suspect something, it was even more stupid to risk everything I have—my husband, my family, my job.

Driving under the delayed effects of two tranquilizers and with frazzled nerves, I realize that I am also putting my life at risk. I park on a side street and cry. My sobs are so loud that someone approaches and asks if I need help. I say no and the person walks away. But the truth is I do need help—a lot. I'm plunging deeper into my inner self, into its sea of mud, and I can't swim.

I'm blinded by hatred. I imagine that Jacob has already recovered from yesterday's dinner and will never want to see me again. It's my fault for wanting to go beyond my limits, for always thinking that my behavior is suspicious, that everyone knows what I am doing. Maybe it's a good idea to call and apologize, but I know he won't answer. Maybe it's better to call my husband and see if he's okay? I know his voice. I know when he's angry and tense, even though he's a master at self-control. But I don't want to know. I'm really scared. My stomach is churning, and my hands clench around the steering wheel. I allow myself to cry as loud as I can, to shout and make a scene in the only safe place on earth: my car. The person who approached me is now eyeing me from afar, afraid I'll do something stupid. No, I won't do anything. I just want to cry. Is that too much to ask?

I feel like I inflicted this abuse on myself. I want to go back in time, only that's impossible. I need to make a plan to regain lost ground, but I can't think straight. All I can do is cry, feeling ashamed and hateful.

How could I have been so naïve? Thinking that Marianne was looking at me and saying what I already knew? Because I felt guilty, like a criminal. I wanted to humiliate her, to destroy her in front of her husband so she wouldn't see me as just a pastime. I know I don't love him, but he has slowly been giving me back some of the joy I'd lost, keeping me from the pit of loneliness I had been drowning in up to my neck. And now I am realizing that those days are gone forever. I have to come back to reality, to the supermarket, to the days that are all alike, and to the safety of my home—something that was once so important to me, but had started feeling like a prison. I need to pick up the pieces that are still left. Perhaps confess everything that happened to my husband.

I know he'll understand. He's a good, intelligent man who always puts family first. But what if he doesn't understand? What if he decides that he's had enough, that we've reached our limit and he's tired of living with a woman who started off complaining of depression and now laments being left by her lover?

My sobbing wanes and I start to think. Work awaits, and I can't spend the whole day sitting in this street filled with the homes of happy couples who have Christmas decorations on their doors, with people coming and going without noticing I'm there. I can't watch my world collapse and not do anything about it.

I need to reflect. I have to draw up a list of priorities. In the coming days, months, and years, will I be able to pretend I'm a devoted wife instead of a wounded animal? Discipline has never been my strong suit, but I can't behave like I'm unstable.

I dry my tears and look straight ahead. Time to start the car? Not yet. I wait a bit longer. If there is one reason to be happy about what happened, it's that I was tired of living a lie. How long before my husband suspected something? Can men tell when their wives fake an orgasm? It's possible, but I have no way of knowing.

I get out of the car and pay for more parking time than necessary. That way I can walk around aimlessly. I call in to work and give a lame excuse: one of the kids had diarrhea and I need to take him to the doctor. My boss believes it; after all, the Swiss don't lie.

But I do lie. I've been lying every day. I've lost my self-respect and I don't know where I'm headed anymore. The Swiss live in the real world. I live in a fantasy one. The Swiss know how to solve their problems. Incapable of solving my own, I created a situation where I had the ideal family and the perfect lover.

I walk through this city that I love, looking at its shops and businesses that—with the exception of places for tourists—seem to have frozen in the fifties and don't have the slightest intention of modernizing. It's cold, but not windy, thank God, which makes the temperature bearable. Trying to distract myself and calm down, I stop in a bookstore, a butcher shop, and a clothing store. Each time I go back out into the street, I feel like the low temperatures are helping put out the bonfire I've become.

Can you train yourself to love the right man? Of course

you can. The problem is forgetting about the wrong man, the one passing by who came in a door that was left open without asking permission.

What exactly did I want from Jacob? I knew from the beginning that our relationship was doomed, although I never imagined it would end in such a humiliating way. Maybe I just wanted what I got: adventure and joy. Or maybe I wanted more—to live with him, to help him grow his career, and to give him the support he no longer seemed to get from his wife and the affection he complained he lacked at one of our first meetings. To pluck him from his home, the way you pluck a flower from someone else's garden, and plant him on my land, even though I know flowers can't survive being treated that way.

I'm hit with a wave of jealousy, but this time there are no tears, just anger. I stop walking and sit on a bench at a random bus stop. I watch the people coming and going, all so busy in their own worlds, tiny enough to fit on the screen of the smartphones from which they are unable to unglue their eyes and ears.

Buses come and go. People get off and walk quickly, maybe because of the cold. Others board slowly, not wanting to get home, to work, or to school. But no one shows any anger or enthusiasm; they're not happy or sad, just poor souls mechanically carrying out the mission that the universe assigned on the day they were born.

After a while I manage to relax a little. I've figured out a few pieces of my inner puzzle. One of them is the reason why this hatred comes and goes, like the buses at this stop. I may have lost the thing that's most important to me in life: my family. I've been defeated in the battle to find happiness, and this not only humiliates me, it keeps me from seeing the way forward.

And my husband? I need to have a frank conversation with him tonight and confess everything. I feel like this will set me free, even if I have to suffer the consequences. I'm tired of lying—to him, to my boss, to myself.

I just don't want to think about this now. More than anything else, it's jealousy that eats away at my thoughts. I can't get up from this bus stop because it's as though there are chains attached to my body. They are heavy and difficult to haul around.

You mean she likes hearing stories about his infidelities while she's in bed with her husband and doing the same things he did with me? I should have realized he had other women when he took the condom from the nightstand. I should have known I was just one more by the way he took me. Many times I left that damn hotel feeling that way, telling myself I wouldn't see him again—all the while aware that this was just another one of my lies and that if he called, I would always be ready, whenever and wherever he wanted.

Yes, I knew all that. And yet I tried to convince myself I was only looking for sex and some adventure. But it wasn't true. Today I realize that yes, I was in love, despite having denied it on all my sleepless nights and empty days. Madly in love.

I don't know what to do. I guess—in fact, I'm sure—that all married people always have a secret crush. It's forbidden, and flirting with the forbidden is what makes life interesting. But few people take it further; only one in seven, according to the article I read in the newspaper. And I think only one in a hundred is capable of getting confused enough to be carried away by the fantasy, like I did. For most, it's nothing more than a fling, something you know from the beginning won't last long. A little thrill to make sex more erotic and hear "I love you" shouted out at the moment of orgasm. Nothing more.

And what if it had been my husband who'd found a mistress? How would I have reacted? It would have been extreme. I would have said that life is unfair, that I'm worthless, and I'm getting old. I'd have screamed bloody murder, I'd have cried nonstop from jealousy, which would have actually been envy—he can, and I can't. I'd have left, slamming the door behind me, and taken the children to my parents' house. Two or three months later I would have regretted it and tried to find some excuse to go back, imagining he would want the same. After four months, I would be terrified by the possibility of having to start all over again. After five months, I would have found a way to ask to come back "for the children," but it would be too late: he would be living with his mistress, a much younger woman, pretty and full of energy, who had begun to make his life fun again.

The phone rings. My boss asks after my son. I say I'm at a bus stop and can't hear well, but that everything's fine and soon I'll be at the paper.

A terrified person can never see reality, preferring to hide in their fantasies. I can't go on like this for more than an hour. I have to pull myself together. My job is waiting, and it might help me.

I leave the bus stop and start walking back to my car. I look at the dead leaves on the ground. In Paris, they'd have already been swept up, I think. But we're in Geneva, a much wealthier city, and they're still there.

These leaves were once part of a tree, a tree that has now gone to ground to prepare for a season of rest. Did the tree have any consideration for the green cloak that covered it, fed it, and enabled it to breathe? No. Did it think of the insects who lived there and helped pollinate its flowers and keep nature alive? No. The tree just thought about itself; some things, like leaves and insects, are discarded as needed.

I'm like one of those leaves on the city ground, who lived thinking it would be everlasting and died without knowing exactly why; who loved the sun and the moon and who watched those buses and rattling streetcars go by for a long time, and yet no one ever had the courtesy to let her know that winter existed. They lived it up, until one day they began to turn yellow and the tree bid them farewell.

It didn't say "see you later" but "good-bye," knowing the leaves would never be back. And it asked the wind for help loosening them from their branches and carrying them far away. The tree knows it can grow only if it rests. And if it grows, it will be respected. And can produce even more beautiful flowers.

Enough. Work is the best therapy now that I've cried all the tears and thought about everything I needed to think about. But I still can't shake anything.

I get to the street where I parked on autopilot and find a guard in a red and blue uniform scanning my car's license plate with a machine.

"Is this your vehicle?"

Yes.

He continues his work. I say nothing. The scanned plate has already entered the system. It's been sent to the main office to be processed and will generate a letter with the discreet police seal in the cellophane window of an official envelope. I'll have thirty days to pay 100 francs, but I can also challenge the fine and spend 500 francs on lawyers.

"You went over by twenty minutes. The maximum here is half an hour."

I just nod. I see he's surprised—I'm not pleading with him

to stop and saying I'll never do it again, nor did I run to stop him when I saw he was there. I had none of the reactions to which he's accustomed.

A ticket comes out of the machine as if we're in the supermarket. He places it in a plastic envelope (to protect it from the elements) and goes to the windshield to place it behind the wiper. I press the button on my key and the lights flash, indicating that a door was left open.

He realizes the foolishness of what he was about to do, but like me, he's on autopilot. After the sound of the doors being unlocked jolts him, he walks up to me and hands me the ticket. We both leave happy. He didn't have to handle any complaints, and I got a little of what I deserve: a punishment.

I'LL FIND out shortly if my husband is exercising the utmost self-control or if he really doesn't give a damn about what happened.

I get home on time after another day of gathering information about the most trivial things in the world: pilot training, a surplus of Christmas trees on the market, and the introduction of electronic controls at railroad crossings. This made me extremely happy, because I was in no condition, physical or mental, to think much.

I prepare dinner as if this were just another evening among the thousands we've spent together. We spend some time watching TV while the children go up to their rooms, lured by the tablets or video games on which they kill terrorists or soldiers depending on the day.

I put the dishes in the dishwasher. My husband is going to try to put our kids to bed. So far we've only talked about our daily duties. I can't tell if it was always like this and I never noticed, or if it's especially strange today. I'll find out soon.

While he's upstairs, I light the fireplace for the first time this year. Watching the fire soothes me, and although I'm revealing something I expect he already knows, I need all the help I can get. I open a bottle of wine and prepare a plate of assorted cheeses. I take my first sip and stare at the flames. I don't feel anxious or afraid. Enough with this double life. Whatever happens today will be better for me. If our marriage has to end, so be it; it will end on a late autumn day before Christmas, while watching the fireplace and talking like civilized people.

He comes downstairs, sees the scene I've prepared, and asks nothing. He just settles in next to me on the sofa and also watches the fire. He drinks his wine. I get ready to refill his glass, but he waves his hand, indicating it was enough.

I make a stupid comment: the temperature today fell below zero. He nods.

Apparently, I'll have to take the initiative.

I really regret what happened at dinner last night . . .

"It wasn't your fault. That woman is really weird. Please don't invite me to any more things like that."

His voice seems calm. But everyone learns as a child that before the worst storms, there's always a moment when the wind stops and everything seems absolutely normal.

I push the matter. Marianne exhibited the jealousy hiding behind her modern, liberal mask.

"It's true. Jealousy tells us: 'You could lose everything you worked so hard to achieve.' It blinds us to everything else, to the moments we've joyfully experienced, to happy times and the bonds created during those occasions. How is it that hatred can wipe out a couple's entire history?"

He's laying the groundwork for me to say everything I need to say. He continues:

"Everyone has days when they say: 'Well, my life isn't exactly lining up with my expectations.' But if life asked you what you had done for it, what would you say?"

Is that a question for me?

"No. I'm questioning myself. Nothing happens without effort. You have to have faith. And for that, you have to break down the barriers of prejudice, which requires courage. To have courage, you must conquer your fears. And so on and so forth. Let's make peace with our days. We can't forget that life is on our side. It also wants to get better. Let's help it out!"

I pour myself another glass of wine. He puts more wood on the fire. When will I have the courage to confess?

But he doesn't seem to want to let me talk.

"Dreaming isn't as simple as it seems. On the contrary, it can be quite dangerous. When we dream, we put powerful engines in motion and can no longer hide the true meaning of our life from ourselves. When we dream, we also make a choice of what price to pay."

Now. The longer I take, the more suffering I'll cause us both.

I raise my glass, make a toast, and say there is something troubling my soul. He replies that we already talked about this over dinner that night when I opened my heart and told him about my fear of being depressed. I explain that that's not what I'm referring to. He interrupts me and continues his line of thought.

"Going after a dream has a price. It may mean abandoning our habits, it may make us go through hardships, or it may lead us to disappointment, et cetera. But however costly it may be, it is never as high as the price paid by people who didn't live. Because one day they will look back and hear their own heart say: 'I wasted my life.' "

He is not making things any easier. Let's suppose what I have to say isn't nonsense, that it is something tangible, genuine, threatening?

He laughs.

"I controlled the jealousy I feel because of you, and I'm happy with that. You know why? Because I always have to show I'm worthy of your love. I have to fight for our marriage, for our union, in ways that have nothing to do with our children. I love you. I would endure anything, absolutely anything, to always have you by my side. But I can't stop you from leaving one day. So if that day comes, you are free to leave and seek your happiness. My love for you is stronger than anything, and I would never stop you from being happy."

My eyes well up with tears. So far I'm not sure what he's

really saying. If this is just a conversation about jealousy or if he's giving me a message.

"I'm not afraid of loneliness," he continues. "I'm afraid of deluding myself, of looking at reality the way I would like it to be and not how it really is."

He takes my hand.

"You are a blessing in my life. I may not be the best husband in the world, because I hardly ever show my feelings. And I know you need that. I also know that because of this, you might not think you're important to me, you might feel insecure, or things like that. But it's not like that. We should sit in front of the fire and talk about everything except for jealousy. Because I'm not interested in that. Perhaps it would be good to take a trip together, just the two of us? Spend New Year's Eve in a different city or even a place we've already been?"

"But what about the children?"

"I'm sure their grandparents would be delighted to take care of them."

And he concludes:

"When you love each other, you have to be ready for anything. Because love is like a kaleidoscope, the kind we used to play with when we were kids. It's in constant movement and never repeats itself. If you don't understand this, you are condemned to suffer for something that really only exists to make us happy. And you know the worst thing? People like that woman, always worried about what others think of their marriage. That doesn't matter to me. The only thing that counts is what you think."

I rest my head on his shoulder. Everything I had to say has lost its importance. He knows what is going on and is able to deal with the situation in a way I never could.

IT'S SIMPLE; as long as you aren't doing anything illegal, making and losing money on the financial market is allowed."

The former tycoon is trying to maintain his pose as one of the richest men in the world. But his fortune evaporated in less than a year after the big financiers discovered he was selling dreams. I try to show interest in what he's saying. After all, I was the one who asked my boss to drop the series of articles about searching for solutions to stress for good.

It's been one week since I received Jacob's message saying I'd ruined everything. One week since I roamed the streets aimlessly, a moment I would soon be reminded of by the traffic ticket. One week since that conversation with my husband.

"We always have to know how to sell an idea. That is what constitutes success for any individual," continues the former tycoon. "Knowing how to sell what they want."

My dear fellow, despite all your pageantry, your aura of seriousness, and your suite in this luxury hotel; despite this magnificent view, your impeccably tailored suit from London, your smile, and your hair, dyed with utmost care so as to leave just a few white hairs to give the impression of "naturalness"; despite the confidence with which you speak, there is something I understand better than you: going around selling an idea isn't everything. You have to find someone to buy. That goes for business, politics, and love.

I imagine, my dear former millionaire, that you understand what I'm talking about: you have charts, assistants, presentations . . . but what people want are results.

Love also wants results, although everyone insists, no, that the act of loving justifies itself. Is that how it is? I should be walking through the Jardin Anglais, in my fur coat my husband bought when he went to Russia, looking around at the autumn, smiling up at the sky and saying: "I love you, and that's enough." Could that be true?

Of course not. I love, but in return I want something concrete—holding hands, kisses, hot sex, a dream to share, the chance to create a new family and raise my children, the opportunity to grow old alongside the person I love.

"We need a very clear goal for any given step," explains the pathetic figure in front of me with a seemingly confident smile.

I must be verging on madness again. I end up relating everything I hear or read to my emotional situation, even this boring interview with this annoying caricature. I think about it twenty-four hours a day—while I'm walking down the street, or cooking, or spending precious moments of my life listening to things that, rather than offer distraction, push me even deeper into the abyss where I'm plummeting.

"Optimism is contagious . . ."

The former tycoon cannot stop talking, certain that he will convert me and that I'll publish this in the newspaper and his redemption will begin. It's great to interview people like this. We need to ask only one question, and they talk for an hour. Unlike my conversation with the Cuban shaman, this time I'm not paying attention to a single word. The recorder is turned on, and later I'll trim this monologue down to six hundred words, the equivalent of about four minutes of conversation.

Optimism is contagious, he states.

If that were the case, all you would have to do is go to the person you loved with a huge grin, full of plans and ideas, and know how to present the package. Does it work? No. What is really contagious is fear, the constant fear of never finding someone to accompany us to the end of our days. And in the name of this fear we are capable of doing anything, including accepting the wrong person and convincing ourselves that he or she's the one, the only one, who God has placed in our path. In very little time the search for security turns into a heartfelt love, and things become less bitter and difficult. Our feelings can be put in a box and pushed to the back of the closet in our head, where it will remain forever, hidden and invisible.

"Some people say I'm one of the most well-connected men in my country. I know entrepreneurs, politicians, industrialists. What is happening with my companies is temporary. Soon you will witness my comeback."

I'm also a well-connected person, I know the same types of people he knows. But I don't want to prepare a comeback. I just want a civilized ending for one of these "connections."

This is because things that don't end clearly always leave a door open, an unexplored possibility, a chance that everything might still go back to being as it was before. I'm not used to this, but I know a lot of people who love being in this situation.

What am I doing? Comparing economics to love? Trying to establish a connection between the financial world and the emotional world? It's been one week since I last heard from Jacob.

It's also been one week since that night in front of the fireplace, when my relationship with my husband returned to normal. Will the two of us be able to rebuild our marriage?

Until this spring I was a normal person. One day I discovered that everything I had could disappear just like that, and instead of reacting like an intelligent person, I panicked. That led to inertia. Apathy. An inability to react and change. And after many sleepless nights, many days of finding no joy in life, I did exactly what I feared most: I walked the other way, despite the dangers. I know I'm not the only one—people have a tendency for self-destruction. By chance, or because life wanted to test me, I found someone who grabbed me by the hair—

literally and figuratively—and rattled me, shaking off the dust that had been piling up and making me breathe again.

All of it completely false. It's the type of happiness that addicts must find when they do drugs. Sooner or later the effects pass, and the despair becomes even greater.

The former tycoon starts talking about money. I didn't ask anything about it, but he talks anyway. He has an enormous need to say he isn't poor, that he can maintain his lifestyle for decades to come.

I can't stand to be here any longer. I thank him for the interview, turn off the recorder, and go get my coat.

"Are you free this evening? We could get a drink and finish this conversation," he suggests.

It's not the first time this has happened. In fact, it's almost a given with me. Even though Mme König won't admit it, I am pretty and smart and I've used my charm to get certain people to say things they wouldn't normally say to journalists, even after warning them I could publish everything. But the men . . . oh, the men! They do everything they can to hide their weaknesses and any eighteen-year-old girl can manipulate them without much effort.

I thank him for the invitation and say I already have plans for that evening. I'm tempted to ask how his latest girlfriend reacted to the wave of negative press and the collapse of his empire. But I can already imagine, and it's of no interest to the newspaper.

I leave, cross the street, and go to the Jardin Anglais, where, moments ago, I imagined walking. I go to the old-fashioned ice-cream parlor on the corner of Rue du 31 Décembre. I like the name of this street because it always reminds me that sooner or later, another year will end and, once again, I'll make big resolutions for the next.

I order a scoop of pistachio with chocolate. I walk to the pier and eat my ice cream while looking at the symbol of Geneva, its jet of water shooting up in the sky and creating a curtain of droplets before me. Tourists get closer and take photos that will come out poorly lit. Wouldn't it be easier to just buy a postcard?

I have visited many monuments around the world, many of mighty men whose names are long forgotten, but who will remain eternally mounted on their beautiful horses. Of women holding their crowns or swords to the sky, symbolizing victories that no longer appear even in textbooks. Of lone, nameless children carved in stone, their innocence lost forever during the hours and days they were forced to pose for an artist whose name history has also stamped out.

With very few exceptions, in the end a city's landmarks aren't its statues, but unexpected things. When Eiffel built a steel tower for the World's Fair, he never even dreamed it would wind up becoming the symbol of Paris—over the Louvre, the Arc de Triomphe, and its magnificent gardens. An apple represents New York. A not-so-crowded bridge is the symbol of San Francisco. Another bridge, this one over the Tagus, dominates the picture postcards of Lisbon. Barcelona has an unfinished cathedral as its most emblematic monument.

And so it is with Geneva. Lake Léman meets the Rhône River at precisely this point, creating a very strong current. A hydroelectric power station was built here to take advantage of the hydraulic power (we're masters at taking advantage of things), but when the workers returned home and closed the valves, the pressure was too great and the turbines ended up bursting.

Until an engineer had the idea to put a fountain in place, allowing the excess water to run off.

Over time, engineers solved the problem and the fountain became unnecessary. But the city's residents voted in a referendum to keep it. The city already had many fountains, and this one was in the middle of a lake. How could they make it more visible?

That was how the mutant monument was born. Powerful pumps were installed and now an extremely forceful jet shoots out five hundred liters of water per second, at two hundred kilometers per hour. They say, and I've confirmed it, that it can be seen from an airplane at thirty thousand feet. It doesn't have a special name; it's just called Jet d'Eau (jet of water), the city's landmark in spite of all the sculptures of men on horses, heroic women, lonely children.

I once asked Denise, a Swiss scientist, what she thought of the Jet d'Eau.

"Our body is made almost entirely of water, through which electrical discharges pass, communicating information. One such piece of information is called love, and it can interfere with the entire organism. Love is always changing. I think that the Jet d'Eau is the most beautiful monument to love conceived by the art of man, because it is also never the same."

I TAKE my phone and call Jacob's office. Sure, I could dial his personal number, but no. I speak with his assistant and let her know I'm going to meet him.

His assistant knows me. She asks me to hold the line while she confirms. One minute later she returns and says she's sorry, but his schedule is fully booked. Perhaps in the new year? I say no, I need to meet with him right away; it's urgent.

"It's urgent" doesn't always open many doors, but in this case I'm sure my chances are good. This time the assistant takes two minutes. She asks if it could be early next week. I let her know I'll be there in twenty minutes.

I say thank you and hang up.

JACOB asks me to get dressed quickly—after all, his office is a public place, paid for by government money. If someone were to find out, he could go to jail. I carefully study the walls covered with carved wood panels and beautiful frescoes on the ceiling. I'm still lying on the worn leather sofa, completely naked.

He is growing nervous. He's in a suit and tie, looking anxiously at his watch. The lunch hour is over. His personal secretary is already back; she knocked quietly on the door, heard "I'm in a meeting," and didn't insist. Forty minutes have passed since then—along with a few hearings and appointments that have likely been canceled.

When I arrived, Jacob greeted me with three pecks on the cheek and pointed formally to the chair in front of his desk. I didn't need my female intuition to figure out he was scared. What was the reason for this meeting? Don't I understand he has a tight schedule? The parliamentary recess will start soon, and he needs to resolve several important issues. Did I not read the message he sent, saying how his wife is convinced there is something between us? We need to wait a while and let things cool off before we go back to meeting.

"Of course I denied everything. I pretended I was deeply shocked by her insinuations. I said my dignity had been offended. That I was sick of her distrust and that she could ask anyone about my behavior. Wasn't she the one who said jealousy was a sign of inferiority? I did what I could, and she merely replied: 'Stop being silly. I'm not complaining about anything, I'm just saying I found out why you've been so kind and polite lately.' It was—"

I didn't let him finish his sentence. I got up and grabbed

him by the collar. He thought I was going to assault him. But instead I gave him a long kiss. Jacob was completely unresponsive, as he'd been imagining I had come there to do something melodramatic. But I continued kissing his mouth and neck as I undid his tie.

He pushed me away. I slapped him across the face.

"I just need to lock the door first. I've also missed you."

He walked across his office, tastefully decorated with nineteenth-century furniture, and turned the key. When he returned I was already nearly naked, wearing just my panties.

As I ripped off his clothes, he started sucking on my breasts. I moaned with pleasure; he covered my mouth with his hand, but I shook my head and continued moaning quietly.

The whole time, I stopped only once to say: My reputation is at stake, as you can imagine. Don't worry.

I got down on my knees and began to give him oral sex. Again, he held my head, setting the pace—faster and faster. But I didn't want him to come in my mouth. I pushed him away and went to the leather sofa, where I leaned back with my legs spread. He kneeled and started to go down on me. When I had the first orgasm, I bit my hand to keep from screaming. The wave of pleasure felt like it would never end. I continued biting my hand.

Then I called his name, telling him I wanted him inside me and to do anything he wanted. He penetrated me, grabbed me by the shoulders, and shook me like a savage. He pushed my legs up so he could go deeper. The pace increased, but I ordered him not to come yet. I needed more and more and more.

He put me on the floor on all fours, like a dog, hit me, and penetrated me again as I wildly moved my waist. From his stifled groans, I knew that he was ready to come, that he could no longer control himself. I made him withdraw, turned over, and asked him to enter me again while looking into my eyes and saying the dirty things we loved to tell each other whenever we made love. I said the nastiest things a woman can say to a man. He called my name softly, begging me to tell him I loved him. But I just spoke profanities and demanded he treat me like a prostitute, like a stranger, that he use me like a slave, someone who didn't deserve respect.

My entire body was covered in goose bumps. The pleasure came in waves. I came again and again as he controlled himself to prolong it as long as possible. Our bodies collided violently, creating rumblings that he must no longer care if anyone heard through the door.

My eyes locked on him, listening to him repeat my name with each movement; I realized he wasn't wearing a condom and was going to come. Once again I shifted, making him withdraw. I asked him to come on my face, in my mouth, and tell me he loved me.

Jacob did exactly as I said, while I masturbated and came, too. Then he embraced me, put my head on his shoulder, and wiped the corners of my mouth with his hands. He said again, many times, that he loved me and that he had really missed me.

But now he's asking me to get dressed, and I don't budge. He's gone back to being the well-behaved boy who the voters admire. He senses something is wrong, but doesn't know what it is. He begins to realize that I'm not just there because he is an amazing lover.

"What do you want?"

Closure. As much as that breaks my heart and leaves me emotionally in shambles, I need to end it. To look in your eyes and say it's over. Never again.

The suffering I endured this past week was almost unbearable. I cried tears I didn't have and became lost in thoughts of being carried away to the campus where your wife works and committed to the university asylum. I thought I'd failed at everything, except at work and as a mother. I was one step away from life and death at every minute, dreaming about everything we could have had if we were still two teenagers looking into the future together, like the first time. But there came a moment when I understood that I had reached the limits of despair and couldn't go any deeper, and when I looked up there was a single outstretched hand: my husband's.

He must have known, too, but his love was stronger. I tried to be honest and tell him everything to lift that weight off my shoulders, but I didn't need to. He made me see that regardless of the choices I made in life, he would always be by my side and so my burden was light.

I realized I was blaming myself and beating myself up over things he wasn't condemning or even blaming me for. I told myself: "I'm not worthy of this man, he doesn't know who I am."

But he does know. And that's what allows me to get back my self-respect and regain my self-esteem. Because if a man like him wants to stay by my side, a man who would have no difficulty at all finding a new partner the day after separating, it's because I'm worth something; I'm worth a lot.

I discovered I could go back to sleeping by his side without feeling like I was dirty or think I was cheating on him. I felt loved and that I deserved this love.

I get up, gather my clothes, and go to his private bathroom. He knows it's the last time he'll see me naked.

There is a long healing process ahead, I say, when I return. I guess you are feeling the same thing, but I'm sure that all Marianne wants is for this fling to end so she can hug you again with the same love and the same security as before.

"Yes, but she won't tell me anything. She knew what was

going on and she closed herself off even more. She was never affectionate, and now she's like a robot, more devoted to her work than ever. It's her way of running away."

I adjust my skirt, put on my shoes, take a bundle out of my bag, and leave it on his desk.

"What's that?"

Cocaine.

"I didn't know you . . ."

He doesn't need to know anything, I think. He doesn't need to know how far I was willing to go to fight for him, the man I was madly in love with. The passion is still there, but the flame weakens each day. I know it will eventually die out completely. Any breakup is painful, and I can feel this pain in every fiber of my body. It's the last time I will see him alone. We will meet again at galas and cocktail parties, at elections and press conferences, but we will never again be the way we were today. It was great to have made love like that and end as we began, both of us completely surrendered to the other. I knew it was the last time; he didn't, but I couldn't say anything.

"What am I supposed to do with it?"

Throw it away. It cost me a small fortune, but throw it away. Then you'll set me free from my addiction.

I don't explain exactly what addiction I'm talking about. It has a name: Jacob König.

I see his expression of surprise and smile. I say good-bye with three kisses on the cheek and leave. In the vestibule, I turn to his aide and wave. He looks away, pretending to focus on a stack of papers, and just mumbles a good-bye.

When I make it to the sidewalk, I call my husband and tell him I would rather spend New Year's Eve at home, with the children. If he wants to travel, let's do it at Christmas.

LET'S take a walk before dinner?"

I nod yes, but I don't move. I stare at the park across from the hotel and, beyond that, the Jungfrau, perpetually snow-capped and illuminated by the afternoon sun.

The human brain is fascinating; we will forget a scent until we smell it again, we will erase a voice from our memory until we hear it again, and even emotions that seemed buried forever will be awakened when we return to the same place.

I think back to when we were at Interlaken the first time. Back then we stayed at a cheap hotel and hiked from one lake to another, each time like we were discovering a new path. My husband was going to run that crazy marathon that has most of its route in the mountains. I was proud of his adventurous spirit, his desire to conquer the impossible and always demand more and more of his body.

He wasn't the only person crazy enough to do it; people came from all over the world, filling the hotels and socializing in the many bars and restaurants of this small town of five thousand inhabitants. I have no idea how Interlaken is in the winter, but from my window it now seems more empty, more removed.

This time we're staying in a better hotel. We have a beautiful suite. The manager's card is on the table, greeting us and offering us the bottle of champagne that we've already emptied.

He calls my name. I come back to reality and we go downstairs to take a walk through the streets before nightfall.

If he asks me whether or not everything is fine, I'll lie, because I don't want to spoil his happiness. But the truth is that the wounds in my heart are taking a long time to heal. He points out the bench where we sat to have coffee one morning and were approached by a couple of neo-hippie foreigners asking for money. We pass in front of one of the churches as the bells ring, he kisses me and I kiss him back, doing all I can to hide what I feel.

We walk holding hands because of the cold—I hate wearing gloves. We stop at a nice bar and drink a little. We go to the train station. He buys the same souvenir he bought last time—a lighter with the symbol of the city. Back then he smoked and ran marathons.

Today he doesn't smoke and he thinks he gets more and more out of breath each day. He is always panting when we walk quickly and, though he tries to hide it, I've noticed he was more tired than usual when we took that run by the lake in Nyon.

My phone is vibrating. It takes me ages to find it in my purse. When I finally find it, the person has already hung up. The screen shows it was my friend, the one who was depressed and, thanks to medication, is a happy person again today.

"If you want to call her back, I don't mind."

I ask why I should call back. Is he unhappy with my company? Does he want to be interrupted by people who will spend hours on the phone engaged in irrelevant chatter?

He gets irritated with me, too. Maybe it's just the effect of the bottle of champagne, coupled with the two glasses of aquavit. His irritation calms me and puts me more at ease; I am walking alongside a human being, with emotions and feelings.

Interlaken sure is strange without the marathon, I say. It looks like a ghost town.

"There are no ski slopes here."

Nor could there be. We are in the middle of a valley, with very high mountains to either side and lakes at each end.

He orders two glasses of gin. I suggest we change bars, but

he is determined to combat the cold with alcohol. We haven't done this in a long time.

"I know it's only been ten years, but when we were here the first time, I was young. I had ambitions, I liked the open air, and I wouldn't let myself be intimidated by the unknown. Have I changed that much?"

You're only in your thirties. Are you really an old man?

He doesn't answer. He downs his drink in one gulp and stares into space. He is no longer the perfect husband and, oddly enough, this makes me happy.

We leave the bar and walk back to the hotel. Along the way we find a beautiful and charming restaurant, but we've already made reservations elsewhere. It's still early—the sign says dinner service doesn't start until seven p.m.

"Let's have another gin."

Who is this man next to me? Has Interlaken awakened forgotten memories and opened up Pandora's box?

I say nothing. And I begin to be afraid.

I ask if we should cancel our reservation at the Italian restaurant and have dinner here instead.

"It doesn't matter."

It doesn't matter? Is he suddenly feeling everything I went through when he thought I was depressed?

For me it *does* matter. I want to go to the restaurant we booked. The same one where we exchanged vows of love.

"This trip was a terrible idea. I'd rather go back tomorrow. I had good intentions: I wanted to relive the early days of our relationship. But is that even possible? Of course not. We're mature. We're living under pressures that didn't exist before. We need to maintain basic needs like education, healthcare, food. We try to have fun on the weekends because that's what everybody does, and when we don't feel like leaving the house, we think there's something wrong with us."

I never want to. I'd rather do nothing.

"Me, too. But what about our children? They want something else. We can't leave them locked up with their computers. They're too young for that. So we force ourselves to take them somewhere and do the same things our parents did with us, the same thing our grandparents did with our parents. An ordinary life. We're an emotionally well-structured family. If one of us needs help, the other is always ready to do anything."

I understand. Like taking a trip to a place filled with memories, for example.

Another glass of gin. He sits in silence for a while before replying.

"That's right. But do you think memories can fill the present? Not at all. In fact, they're suffocating me. I'm discovering I'm no longer the same person. Until we got here and had that bottle of champagne, everything was fine. Now I realize just how far I am from living the life I dreamed of when I visited Interlaken the first time."

What did you dream?

"It was silly. But it was still my dream. And I could have made it come true."

But what was it?

"Sell everything I had, buy a boat, and travel the world with you. My father would have been furious that I didn't follow in his footsteps, but it wouldn't have mattered. We'd stop off at ports, do odd jobs until we earned enough to move on, and as soon as we had enough money, we'd set sail again. Be with people we'd never seen before and discover places not listed in the guidebooks. Adventure. My only wish was *adventure.*"

He orders another glass of gin and drinks it at unprecedented speed. I stop drinking because I'm already feeling nauseated; we haven't had anything to eat. I'd like to say that I would have been the happiest woman in the world if he'd gotten his wish. But I had better keep quiet or he'll feel worse.

"Then came the first child."

So? There must be millions of couples with children doing exactly what he suggested.

He reflects a bit.

"I wouldn't say millions. Maybe thousands."

His eyes change; they no longer show aggression, but sadness.

"There are times when we should stop to take a look at the whole picture: our past and our present. What we have learned and the mistakes we made. I was always afraid of those moments. I trick myself, telling myself that I made the best choices and had to make a few small sacrifices. Nothing major."

I suggest we walk a bit. His eyes are starting to get weird, dull.

He slams his fist on the table. The waitress looks frightened, and I order another glass of gin for me. She refuses. It's time to close the bar because dinner will begin soon. And she brings the bill.

I wonder how my husband will react. But he just gets out his wallet and throws some money on the counter. He takes my hand and we go out in the cold.

"I'm afraid that if I think too much about everything that could have been, and never was, I'll fall into a dark hole . . ."

I know that feeling. We talked about this at the restaurant, when I opened up to you.

He doesn't seem to hear.

". . . deep down there's a voice telling me: none of this makes sense. The universe has existed for billions of years, and it will continue to exist after you die. We live in a microscopic part of a gigantic mystery, and we still have no answers to our childhood questions: Is there life on another planet? If God is good, why does He allow suffering and the pain of others? And what's worse: time continues to pass. Often, for no apparent reason, I feel an immense dread. Sometimes it's when I'm at work, sometimes in the car, and sometimes when I put the kids to bed. I look at them lovingly, afraid: What will happen to them? They live in a country that gives us peace and security, but what about the future?"

Yes, I understand what you're saying. I imagine we're not the only ones to think that way.

"Then I see you making breakfast or dinner and occasionally I think that fifty years from now, or maybe even less, one of us will be sleeping alone, crying every night because once we were happy. The children will be all grown up and far away. The surviving one of us will be sick, always needing help from strangers."

He stops talking, and we walk in silence. We pass by a sign announcing a New Year's Eve party. He kicks it violently. Two or three passersby look at us.

"Forgive me. I didn't mean to say all that. I brought you here to make you feel better without all the daily pressures. Blame it on the booze."

I'm stunned.

We pass by a group of young men and women who are talking animatedly among the beer cans scattered everywhere. My husband, usually shy and serious, approaches them and invites them to have another drink.

The young people look frightened. I apologize, hinting that we're both drunk and one drop more of alcohol might lead to catastrophe. I grab his arm and we carry on.

How long has it been since I've done that? He was always the protector, the helper, the problem solver. Now I'm the one trying to keep him from skidding and falling. His mood has changed again, and now he's singing a song I've never heard—perhaps a traditional song of that region.

When we approach the church, the bells ring again.

That's a good sign, I say.

"I listen to the bells. They speak of God. But is God listening to us? We're in our thirties, and life isn't fun anymore. If not for our children, what would be the point of all this?"

I prepare myself to say something. But I have no answer. We arrive at the restaurant where we exchanged our first words of love and have a depressing candlelight dinner in one of the most beautiful and most expensive cities in Switzerland.

WHEN I awake, there's already daylight outside. I had a dreamless sleep and didn't wake up in the middle of the night. I look at the clock: nine a.m.

My husband is still sleeping. I go to the bathroom, brush my teeth, and order breakfast for the two of us. I put on a robe and go to the window to pass the time while I wait for the room service to arrive.

At this point, I notice something: the sky is full of paragliders! They land in the park opposite the hotel. Most are not alone, and have an instructor behind them steering. First-timers.

How can they do such a crazy thing? Have we reached the point where risking our life is the only thing that frees us from boredom?

Another paraglider lands. And another. Friends film everything, smiling cheerfully. I wonder what the view must be like up there, because the mountains surrounding us are very, very high.

Although I envy every one of those people, I would never have the courage to jump.

The doorbell rings. The waiter enters with a silver tray, a vase with a rose, coffee (for my husband), tea (for me), croissants, hot toast, rye bread, jams of various flavors, eggs, orange juice, the local newspaper, and everything else that makes us happy.

I wake him up with a kiss. I don't remember the last time I did that. He is startled, but then smiles. We sit at the table and savor the treats in front of us. We talk a bit about our drinking spree last night.

"I think I needed that. But don't take what I said too seriously. When a balloon bursts, it startles everyone, but it's nothing more than that: a bursting balloon. Harmless."

I want to say it felt great to discover all his weaknesses, but I just smile and keep eating my croissant.

He also notices the paragliders. His eyes light up. We get dressed and go downstairs to enjoy the morning.

We go straight to the front desk. He says we'll be leaving today, asks them to bring down our suitcases, and pays the bill.

Are you sure? Can't we stay until tomorrow morning?

"I'm sure. Last night was enough for me to understand that it's impossible to go back in time."

We head to the door crossing the long, glass-ceilinged lobby. I read in one of the brochures that there used to be a street here; now they've joined the two buildings that stood on either side. Tourism is apparently thriving, even without ski slopes.

But instead of going out the door, my husband turns left and approaches the concierge.

"How can we go paragliding?"

We? I don't have the slightest intention of doing that.

The concierge hands him a brochure. It's all there.

"And how do we get up top?"

The concierge explains that we don't have to go all the way up. The road is very treacherous. All we have to do is set a time and they'll pick us up from the hotel.

Isn't it very dangerous? Jumping into the nothing between two mountain ranges without ever having done it before? Who is in charge? Are there any government controls on the instructors and their equipment?

"Madam, I've been working here for ten years. I paraglide at least once a year. I've never seen a single accident."

He is smiling. He must have repeated those words thousands of times over those ten years.

"Shall we?"

What? Why don't you go alone?

"Sure, I can go by myself. You can wait for me down here with the camera. But I need and want to have this experience in life. It's always terrified me. Just yesterday we talked about when everything gets stuck in a rut and how we no longer test our limits. It was a very sad night for me."

I know. He asks the concierge to set a time.

"Now, this morning, or in the afternoon, when you can see the sunset reflected on the surrounding snow?"

Now, I reply.

"So, will it be one person or two?"

Two, if we do it now. If I don't have a chance to think about what I'm doing. If I don't have time to open the box and let the demons out—fear of heights, of the unknown, of death, of life, of extreme feelings. Now or never.

"We have the option of twenty-minute, half-hour, and one-hour flights."

Are there ten-minute flights?

No.

"Would you like to jump from one thousand three hundred and fifty or one thousand eight hundred meters?"

I'm already starting to back down. I didn't need all this information. Of course I want the lowest possible jump.

"Darling, that makes no sense. I'm sure nothing will happen, but if it did, the danger is the same. Falling from twenty-one meters, or the equivalent of the seventh floor of a building, would have just the same consequences."

The concierge laughs. I laugh to hide my feelings. How could I have been so naïve to think that a measly five hundred meters would make any difference?

The concierge picks up the phone and talks to someone.

"There is only space available for jumps at one thousand three hundred and fifty meters."

More absurd than my earlier fear is the relief I feel now. Oh, good!

The car will be at the hotel doorstep in ten minutes.

I STAND before the chasm with my husband and five or six other people, waiting for my turn. On the way up I thought about my children and the possibility of losing their parents . . . Then I realized we wouldn't be jumping together.

We put on special thermal outfits and helmets. Why the helmet? So my skull will still be intact if I hit a rock and skip three thousand feet to the ground?

The helmet is mandatory.

Perfect. I put on the helmet—just like the ones worn by cyclists on the streets of Geneva. Completely stupid, but I won't argue.

I look ahead; between us and the chasm is a snow-covered slope. I can stop the flight in the first second by landing there and walking back up. I don't have to go all the way to the end.

I've never been afraid of flying. It's always been a part of my life. But the thing is, when we're in a plane, it doesn't occur to us that it's exactly the same as going paragliding. The only difference is that the metal cocoon feels like a shield and gives us the feeling that we're protected. That's it.

That's it? In my meager understanding of the laws of aerodynamics, I suppose so.

I need to convince myself. I need a better argument.

This is a better argument; the airplane is made of metal. It's extremely heavy. And it carries luggage, people, equipment, and tons of explosive fuel. The paraglider, in turn, is light, descends with the wind, and obeys the laws of nature like a leaf falling from a tree. It makes much more sense.

"Do you want to go first?"

Yes, I do. Because if something happens to me, you'll know

and can take care of our children. And you'll feel guilty for the rest of your life for having this insane idea. I will be remembered as a companion for all seasons, one who always stood by her husband's side, in sorrow and in joy, adventure and routine.

"We're ready, madam."

Are you the instructor? Aren't you too young for this? I'd rather go with your boss. It's my first time, after all.

"I've been jumping since I reached the age minimum of sixteen. I've been jumping for five years, not just here, but many different places around the world. Don't worry, madam."

His condescending tone annoys me. Old people and their fears should be respected. Besides, he must tell everybody that.

"Remember the instructions. And when we start to run, don't stop. Let me take care of the rest."

Instructions. As if we were now familiar with all of this, when the most they had the patience to explain was that the risk lies exactly in wanting to stop in the middle. And that, when we reach the ground, we should keep walking until we feel our feet firmly fixed.

My dream: feet on the ground. I go to my husband and ask him to go last, then he'll have time to see what happens to me.

"Want to bring the camera?" asks the instructor.

The camera can be attached to an aluminum rod approximately two feet long. No, I do not. For starters, I'm not doing this to show other people. And even if I can overcome my panic, I'd be more worried about filming than admiring the scenery. I learned that with my dad when I was a teenager: we hiked the Matterhorn and I stopped every minute to take pictures until he fumed: "Do you think all this beauty and grandeur can fit in a little square of film? Record things in your heart. It's more important than trying to show people what you're experiencing."

My flight partner, in all his wisdom of twenty-one years,

begins attaching ropes to my body with big aluminum clips. The chair is attached to the glider; I will go in front, he in the back. I can still give up, but that's no longer me. I am completely unresponsive.

The twenty-one-year-old veteran and the ringleader trade opinions about the wind as we get into position.

He also fastens himself to the chair. I can feel his breath on the back of my head. I look behind me and I don't like what I see: a row of colored pieces of fabric stretches across the white snowy ground, each with a person tied to it. At the end of the row is my husband, also wearing a bicycle helmet. I guess he had no choice and will jump two or three minutes after me.

"We're ready. Start running."

I don't move.

"Let's go. Start running."

I explain that I don't want to keep twirling around in the sky. Let's go down gently. Five minutes of flight is good for me.

"You can let me know while we're flying. But, please, there's a line. We have to jump now."

As I no longer have free will, I follow orders. I start running toward the void.

"Faster."

I go faster, my boots kicking snow in all directions. Actually, it's not me who is running, but a robot who obeys voice commands. I start to scream—not from fear or excitement, but from instinct. I've gone back to being a cave woman, like the Cuban shaman said. We're afraid of spiders and insects, and we scream in situations like this. We've always screamed.

Suddenly my feet lift off the ground, and I hold on to the belts securing me to the chair with all my might. I stop screaming. The instructor keeps running for a few more seconds and then immediately we're no longer going in a straight line. The wind is controlling our lives.

I don't open my eyes that first minute—I don't want a concept of height, the mountains, the danger. I try to imagine that I'm at home in the kitchen, telling the kids a story about something that happened during our trip; maybe about the town, or maybe about the hotel room. I can't tell them their father drank so much he fell down when we were headed back to the hotel. I can't say I took a risk and went flying, because they'll want to do it, too. Or, worse, they might try to fly alone and throw themselves from the top floor of our house.

Then I realize I'm being stupid; why be here with my eyes closed? No one made me jump. *"I've been here for ten years and have never seen a single accident,"* said the concierge.

I open my eyes.

And what I see, what I feel, is something I will never be able to accurately describe. Down below is the valley linking the two lakes, and the town between them. I'm flying, free in space and silence as we follow the wind, sailing in circles. The mountains surrounding us no longer seem so high or threatening, but friendly, dressed in white, with the sun glistening all around.

My hands relax, I let go of the straps, and I open my arms like a bird. The man behind me must have realized that I'm a different person. Instead of continuing down, he starts to rise, using invisible currents of warm air in what once seemed like a homogeneous atmosphere.

Ahead of us is an eagle, sailing the same ocean and effortlessly using its wings to control its mysterious flight. Where does it want to go? Is it just having fun, enjoying life and the beauty all around it?

It feels like I'm communicating with the eagle by telepathy. The flight instructor follows it, our guide. Show us where we need to go to climb increasingly skyward—to fly forever. I feel the same thing I felt that day in Nyon when I imagined running until my body couldn't run anymore.

And the eagle tells me: "Come. You are heaven and earth, the wind and the clouds, the snow and the lakes."

It seems like I am in my mother's womb, completely safe and protected and experiencing things for the first time. Soon I will be born, and I will turn back into a human being who walks with two feet on the face of the Earth. At the moment, though, all I am doing is existing in this womb, putting up no resistance and letting myself go wherever I'm taken.

I'm free.

Yes, I'm free. And the eagle is right: I am the mountains and the lakes. I have no past, present, or future. I am getting to know what people call 'Eternity."

For a split second I wonder: Does everyone who jumps have this same feeling? But what does that matter? I don't want to think about others. I'm floating in Eternity. Nature speaks to me as if I were its beloved daughter. The mountain tells me: "You have my strength." The lakes tell me: "You have my peace and my calm." The sun tells me: "Shine like me, go beyond yourself. Listen."

I start to hear the voices that have been stifled inside for so long, stifled by haunting thoughts, by loneliness, by night terrors, the fear of change, and the fear that everything will stay the same. The higher we go, the further I distance myself from me.

I'm in another world where things fall perfectly into place. Far from that life full of chores to do, impossible desires, suffering, and pleasure. I have nothing and I am everything.

The eagle begins to turn toward the valley. With open arms

I mimic the movement of its wings. If anyone could see me right now, they wouldn't know who I am, because I am light, space, and time. I'm in another world.

And the eagle tells me: "This is Eternity."

In Eternity, we don't exist; we are just an instrument of the Hand that created the mountains, the snow, the lakes, and the sun. I go back in time and space to the moment when everything is created and the stars walk backward. I want to serve this Hand.

Several ideas appear and disappear without changing the way I feel. My mind has left my body and blended with nature. Oh, what a pity the eagle and I must land at the park across from the hotel down below. But what does it matter what will happen in the future? I am here, in this womb made of nothing and everything.

My heart fills every corner of the universe. I try to explain this to myself in words, try to find a way to remember what I feel right now, but soon these thoughts disappear and emptiness returns to fill everything once again.

My heart!

Before I saw a gigantic universe around me; and now the universe seems like a little dot within my heart that has infinitely expanded, like space. An instrument. A blessing. My mind struggles to maintain control and explain at least something that I'm feeling, but the power is stronger.

Power. The feeling of Eternity gives me a mysterious feeling of power. I can do anything, even end world suffering. I am flying and talking with the angels, hearing voices and revelations that will soon be forgotten, but that, at this moment, are as real as the eagle before me. I will never be capable of explaining what I feel, not even to myself, but what does it matter? It's the future, and I'm not there yet. I'm in the present.

The rational mind disappears again and I am grateful. I

bow to my gigantic heart filled with light and power, which can encompass everything that has already happened and what will happen from now until the end of time.

For the first time I hear something: dogs barking. We are nearing the ground and reality begins to return. In a moment I will be stepping on the planet where I live, but in my heart I have experienced all the planets and all the suns, which was greater than anything.

I want to stay in this state, but my thoughts are returning. I see our hotel to the right. The lakes are already hidden by the forests and small hills.

My God, can't I stay this way forever?

"You cannot," says the eagle, who led us to the park where we will land shortly, and who now bids us farewell because it has found a new stream of warm air. It climbs up again effortlessly, without battings its wings, and controls the wind with its feathers. "If you stayed this way forever, you couldn't live in this world," it says.

So what? I begin to argue with the eagle, but I find that I am doing it rationally, trying to reason. How will I live in this world after having gone through what I did in Eternity?

"Find a way," replies the eagle, almost inaudibly. Then it departs—forever—from my life.

The instructor whispers something—he reminds me that I have to run when my feet hit the ground.

I see the grass in front of me. The thing I had so yearned for before—reaching solid ground—has now turned into the end of something.

Of what, exactly?

My feet hit the ground. I run a little, and the instructor controls the paraglider. Then he comes up to me and loosens the chains. He looks at me. I gaze at the sky. All I can see are other colorful paragliders, approaching where I am.

I realize that I am crying.

"Are you all right?"

I nod yes. I don't know if he understands what I experienced up there.

Yes, he understands. He says that once a year he flies with someone who has the same reaction as me.

"When I ask what it is, they aren't able to explain it. The same thing happens to my friends; some people go into a state of shock and they only recover when their feet touch the ground."

It's exactly the opposite. But I don't feel like explaining anything.

I thank him for his comforting words. I would like to explain that I never wanted what I experienced up there to end. But it's over, and I have no obligation to sit here explaining anything to anyone. I walk away to sit on one of the park benches and wait for my husband.

I can't stop crying. He lands, approaches me with a big grin, and says it was a fantastic experience. I keep crying. He hugs me, says it's all over now, and that he shouldn't have made me do something I didn't want to.

It's not that at all, I say. Just leave me alone, please. I'll be fine in a little while.

Someone from the support team comes to collect our outfits and special shoes and hands us our coats. I do everything automatically, but my every move brings me back to a different world, the one we call the "real" world, the one where I don't want to be at all.

But I have no choice. The only thing I can do is ask my husband to leave me alone for a while. He asks if we should go back to the hotel because it's cold. No, I'm fine right here.

I sit there for half an hour, crying. Tears of bliss that wash my soul. Finally, I realize that it is time to return to the world for good.

I get up. We go to the hotel, get our car, and my husband drives back to Geneva. The radio is on so no one feels compelled to talk. I gradually begin to get a terrible headache, but I know what it is: my blood returning to parts that were blocked by emotions that are finally beginning to dissolve. The moment of release is accompanied by pain, but it's always been that way.

He doesn't need to explain what he said yesterday. I don't need to explain what I felt today.

The world is perfect.

IN JUST one hour the year will come to an end. The city decided on significant spending cuts for Geneva's traditional New Year's Eve celebrations, so we will have fewer fireworks. It's just as well; I've seen fireworks my whole life and they no longer give me the same thrill as they did when I was a child.

I cannot say I am going to miss these past 365 days. The wind blew, lightning struck, and the sea nearly capsized my boat, but in the end I managed to cross the ocean and reach dry land.

Dry land? No relationship should go off in search of that. What kills a relationship between two people is precisely the lack of challenge, the feeling that nothing is new anymore. We need to continue to be a surprise for each other.

It all begins with a big party. Friends come out, the celebrant says things he's repeated at hundreds of weddings, like that idea of building a house on rock, and not on sand. The guests throw rice; we throw the bouquet. The single women secretly envy us, and the married women know we are starting on a path that is not at all like what we've read about in fairy tales.

And then reality gradually begins to set in, but we don't accept it. We want our partner to remain the person we met at the altar and with whom we exchanged rings. As if we could stop time.

We cannot. We should not. Wisdom and experience don't change the man. Time doesn't change the man. The only thing that changes us is love. While I was in the air, I understood that my love for life, for the universe, was more powerful than anything.

I REMEMBER a sermon written by a young unknown nineteenth-century pastor analyzing the Epistle of Saint Paul to the Corinthians and the various sides that Love reveals as it grows. He tells us that many of the spiritual texts we see today are addressed to only one part of man.

They offer Peace, but do not speak of Life.

They discuss Faith, but forget Love.

They tell us about Justice, and do not mention Revelation, like the one I had when I jumped from the precipice in Interlaken and the one that got me out of the black hole I had dug in my soul.

May it always be clear that only True Love can compete with any other Love in this world. When we give everything, we have nothing more to lose. And then fear, jealousy, boredom, and monotony disappear, and all that remains is the light from a void that does not frighten us, but brings us closer to one another. The light that always changes, and that is what makes it beautiful and full of surprises—not always those we hope for, but those we can live with.

To love abundantly is to live abundantly.

To love forever is to live forever. Eternal life is coupled with Love.

Why do we want to live forever? Because we want to live another day with this person by our side. Because we want to keep going with someone who deserves our Love, and who knows how to love us as we think we deserve to be loved.

Because living is loving.

Even Love for a pet—a dog, for example—can justify the life of a human being. If he no longer has this bond of Love in his life, any reason to keep on living also disappears.

Let us first seek Love, and everything else will be added.

During these ten years of marriage, I have enjoyed almost every pleasure a woman can have, and had to bear things I did not deserve. Yet when I look back, there were only a few moments—usually very short—when I was able to find even a poor imitation of what I imagine True Love to be: the birth of my children, when I sat holding hands with my husband and looking at the Alps, or the enormous jet of water in Lake Geneva. But these few moments are what justify my existence, because they give me the strength to keep going and bring joy to my days—no matter how much I tried to bring them sorrow.

I go to the window and look at the city outside. The snow they had promised did not fall. Still, I think this is one of the most romantic New Year's Eves I have ever had, because I was dying and Love revived me. Love, the only thing that will remain when the human race has died out.

Love. My eyes well up with tears of joy. No one can force himself to love, nor can he force another person. All you can do is look at Love, fall in love with Love, and imitate it.

There is no other way to achieve love and there is no mystery about it. We love others, we love ourselves, we love our enemies, and then we will never want for anything in our lives. I can turn on the television and see what is happening around the world because, as long as a bit of Love exists in these tragedies, we are heading for salvation. Because Love begets more Love.

Those who know how to love, love Truth, rejoice with the Truth, and do not fear it, because sooner or later it redeems everything. They seek the Truth with a clear, humble mind lacking prejudice or intolerance—and are ultimately satisfied with what they find.

Perhaps the word "sincerity" isn't the best way to explain this characteristic of Love, but I can't find any other. I'm not talking about the sincerity that demeans those close to you; True Love does not consist of exposing your weaknesses to others, but instead of being unafraid to show when you need help and rejoicing in finding that things are better than what others said.

I think fondly of Jacob and Marianne. Unwittingly, they brought me back to my husband and my family. I hope they are happy on this last night of the year, and that all this also brought them closer together.

Am I trying to justify my adultery? No. I sought Truth and I found it. I hope it's like that for everyone who has had this experience.

Learn to love better.

This should be our goal in the world: learn to love.

Life offers us thousands of opportunities for learning. Every man and every woman, in every day of our lives, always has a good opportunity to surrender to Love. Life is not a long vacation, but a constant learning process.

And the most important lesson is learning to love.

Loving better and better. Because the languages, the countries, the solid Swiss Confederation, Geneva and the street where I live with its lampposts, our house, the living-room furniture, it will all disappear . . . and my body will disappear, too.

But one thing will be forever marked on the soul of the universe: my Love. All in spite of my mistakes, my decisions that caused others to suffer, and the moments when I thought it didn't exist.

I LEAVE the window and call out to my children and husband. I say that—according to tradition—we have to climb up on the sofa in front of the fireplace and, exactly at midnight, step on the floor with our right foot.

"Darling, it's snowing!"

I rush to the window again and look at the light of one of the streetlamps. Yes, it's snowing! How had I not noticed before?

"Can we go outside?" asks one of the children.

Not yet. First we will climb on the sofa, eat twelve grapes, and save the seeds to have prosperity all year long. We will do everything we learned from our ancestors.

Then we will go outside to celebrate life. I am sure that the new year will be excellent.

Geneva, November 30, 2013

A NOTE ABOUT THE AUTHOR

One of the most influential writers of our time, Paulo Coelho is the author of many international best sellers, including *The Alchemist, Aleph, Eleven Minutes,* and *Manuscript Found in Accra.* Translated into 80 languages, his books have sold more than 165 million copies in more than 170 countries. He is a member of the Brazilian Academy of Letters and has received the Chevalier de l'Ordre National de la Légion d'Honneur. In 2007 he was named a United Nations Messenger of Peace.

A NOTE ON THE TYPE

This book was set in a typeface called Berling, a roman font with the characteristics of an old face. This distinguished letter is a computer version of the original type designed by the Swedish typographer Karl Erik Forsberg (born 1914). Forsberg is best known for designing Berling—named after the foundry that produced it, Berlingska Stilgjuteriet of Lund.

Typeset by Scribe, Philadelphia, Pennsylvania

Printed and bound by Berryville Graphics, Berryville, Virginia

Designed by Claudia Martinez